ANIMAL RESCUE TEAM

Special Delivery!

SUE STAUFFACHER

ANIMAL RESCUE TEAM

Special Delivery!

THIS IS A BORZOI BOOK PUBLISHED BY ALFRED A. KNOPF

Visit us on the Web! www.randomhouse.com/kids

Educators and librarians, for a variety of teaching tools, visit us at www.randomhouse.com/teachers

Library of Congress Cataloging-in-Publication Data
Stauffacher, Sue.
Special delivery! / by Sue Stauffacher; illustrated by Priscilla Lamont. — 1st ed.
    p.   cm. — (Animal Rescue Team)
Summary: Ten-year-old Keisha and her family's animal rescue center face more challenges involving a baby crow in a mailbox and a skunk found in the nearby community garden.
ISBN 978-0-375-85848-2 (trade) — ISBN 978-0-375-95848-9 (lib. bdg.) — ISBN 978-0-375-89540-1 (e-book)
[1. Skunks—Fiction. 2. Crows—Fiction. 3. Animal rescue—Fiction. 4. Family life—Fiction. 5. Racially mixed people—Fiction.] I. Lamont, Priscilla, ill. II. Title.
PZ7.S8055Spe 2010
[Fic]—dc22
2009023174

Printed in the United States of America
July 2010
10 9 8 7 6 5 4 3 2 1
First Edition

For my nephew, Matt Hutchins, a real comedian

Chapter 1

At ten, Keisha Carter, the oldest Carter child, knew about a lot of things. But she did not know what ricotta was, and she did not want to ask. In the container on the counter, it had looked suspiciously like cottage cheese. In Keisha's experience, cottage cheese was lumpy and yucky. It was very hard to sit at the intake desk and feel hungry for the pancakes Grandma Alice was making, which Keisha could now hear sizzling in the pan, and imagine cottage cheese inside them.

Normally, Grandma staffed the intake desk at Carters' Urban Rescue in the mornings, but she was better at pancakes than Keisha, and Mama and Daddy were trying to get an enclosure ready for a pair of injured ducklings that had been found by a fisherman at the Grand River boat launch.

Keisha was almost glad when the phone rang because then she didn't have to think about her breakfast being ruined by cottage cheese's evil twin—ricotta.

"Carters' Urban Rescue," Keisha said in her grown-up voice (the very same voice she used when counting double Dutch).

"Is this Carters' Urban Rescue?" Keisha heard a

man's voice along with a bunch of crackly and windy noises.

"Yes."

"Sorry. You're breaking up. Is this the place where you report wild animals?"

"It depends on what they've done," Keisha said. "If they've broken the law, you should call the police department."

Of course, this wasn't true. Keisha was using one of her father's jokes. The person at the other end of the line did not laugh.

Keisha heard more whistling sounds and also what sounded like water splashing on the ground. She really didn't like it when people called her from the great outdoors because it was so hard to hear.

"I'm over here at the community garden," the man shouted into the phone. "It smells awful! A skunk has been here and left a trail of his stinky skunk stuff."

"Do you mean the skunk sprayed?" Keisha asked.

"Hold on, hold on. Jane's got a point to make." The phone got all muffly as if the man who was talking had pressed it to his chest.

The community garden sat next to Hillcrest School. It was a big flat area that used to be a baseball diamond, but the school had closed and the city had turned it into a community garden. Keisha loved to ride her bike past it and look at the sunflowers. By this late in summer, they were taller than Daddy. And Daddy was taller than almost everything.

Keisha heard a scraping noise. The caller had put the phone back to his ear. "My wife, Jane—Mrs. Peters—saw the skunk yesterday afternoon strolling through the nasturtiums. She thought it was odd at the time. And then this morning when Jane and I came to get our tools, all the other gardeners were standing around the shed with their noses plugged. Talk about making a stink! And it was coming from inside the shed. *That's* where he did it."

"And you're sure it was skunk spray?"

"Sure I'm sure. When I was a kid, I got sprayed by a skunk. My mother washed me in a bathtub of tomato juice. Who could forget that?"

It was Keisha's job—or anyone's job who sat at the intake desk—to figure out if the people who called Carters' Urban Rescue had a real problem that needed attention or they just needed information about what to do next. A problem meant that someone from Carters' Urban Rescue drove over in the old truck to check out the situation. A question meant that no visit would be made, but Keisha might be able to educate the man on the other end of the line to help himself.

As far as possible, the Carters liked to help people

take care of their own problems. Besides, today was a very busy day because at 4 p.m., her little brother Razi was going to become the next new member of their 4-H Wild 4-Ever Club. You couldn't be a member until you turned six. And Razi had turned six last month.

Keeping the phone pressed to her ear, she pulled the skunk file out of the drawer with her right hand and an intake form out with her left. Even if the Carters didn't go out to the community garden, they still needed to know who called about what. Mama was very clear about this.

"Just a few questions," she said. "Can I have your name and telephone number?"

"Peters, Albert Peters. Five-five-five six-two-seven-four. Look, it says here in the phone book Carters' Urban Rescue. All I'm asking is, come out and rescue us from this skunk!"

"Usually, it's wildlife we rescue, not people, Mr. Peters." Keisha paged through her skunk file. "It's strange that a skunk would spray in its own den," she said. "You're sure no one else saw it? Skunks usually have a reason to spray."

"You don't need to see a skunk, miss, to know where it's been. Jane thinks he dug a hole under the shed. She's showing me the dirt right now. Yup. There it is."

4

Keisha didn't want to sound too big for her britches by telling Mr. Peters many animals could have made that hole. Foxes, groundhogs and ground squirrels dug holes. Her brother Razi dug holes. Even baby Paulo could make a serious hole if you set him in the sandbox after breakfast with a soupspoon.

"I have an idea, Mr. Peters."

"Well, give it to me, young lady, because I am fresh out of ideas . . . and I'm starting to get a headache."

"If that skunk was traveling through the garden, it won't be back to spray again. But if . . . if it is living there like you think, there's a way to find out."

"I'm all ears."

"All you have to do is sprinkle a fine coating of flour around that den you found and look at it tomorrow morning. If you find little paw prints, call us up and we'll help you identify them."

"Flour, you say. Do you provide that or do we?"

"Well, it would help if you did, Mr. Peters. Carters' Urban Rescue is a not-for-profit organization."

"All right, then. We have our marching orders. Jane makes an excellent apple tart. I'm sure she won't mind sacrificing a little flour to the effort. In the meantime, I'll finish watering my tomatoes with one hand and pinching my nose with the other."

As Keisha hung up the phone, Grandma Alice passed the desk with a plate of steaming pancakes. "Breakfast!" she shouted out the door.

It was as if the whole Carter family had been sitting outside the back door waiting for Alice to call. Keisha pushed the button that transferred the ringing phone right to the voice mail and headed to the bathroom to wash her hands.

Before the water was warm, Razi pushed his head through the circle of Keisha's arms and said: "Me first."

Razi was just about to start first grade. Keisha felt a little sorry for Mrs. Jenkins, who would be his teacher. A few months into kindergarten last year, the teachers had presented Mama with the All-Day Razi Award. Half days with Razi could be a challenge, so the teachers felt taking care of Razi 24/7 deserved a special certificate.

"You can't be first because my hands are already clean," Keisha said, taking Razi's hands between hers and helping him rub-a-dub-dub them clean.

"Ugh. Your fingernails, Razi."

"We were looking for snails and grubs for the ducks."

Keisha grabbed a towel and dried Razi's hands before he could wave them all over the floor. He tugged away from her and rushed to the table.

Baby Paulo wasn't dirty. Though he was big for almost one and a half, he could still ride with Mama in the sling. You didn't get very dirty if you were pressed up against Mama. She set him in the high chair and swiped his hands with the dishcloth. Alice put the big steaming plate of pancakes in the middle of the table.

Keisha leaned forward to see if lumps of ricotta cheese poked through. She tried not to be obvious about it. Alice didn't like anyone inspecting the food. Daddy was serving Keisha three pancakes—her normal amount.

She might have to fake it.

"The secret here, according to Chef O's TV show, is to beat the egg whites and the ricotta separately and then fold them together." Grandma Alice watched Chef O's show every Tuesday night on GRTV. Chef O said every day should be a celebration and every meal should be a party.

"Don't forget my parasol," Alice said as Mama poured her pomegranate juice. Grandma took Chef O very seriously.

"One parasol coming right up." Daddy dropped a little paper umbrella in Grandma's juice. "Did you take that phone call, Mom?"

"I took it, Daddy." Keisha poured maple syrup over

her pancakes and cut off a small bite with her fork. . . . Still no ricotta in sight.

"Mr. Peters at the community garden thinks there's a skunk living under the shed where they keep the tools. He says it sprayed last night."

"Did they see a skunk? How do they know?"

"Because it has a stripey on its back." Razi was eating his pancakes the Nigerian way by tearing off strips and dipping them in his syrup. As long as hands were clean, Carter children could eat either way: with their fingers, like Mama's family from Nigeria, or like Daddy's family from Chicago by way of Sweden did with their forks. But that rule was only for meals at home.

"The usual way. He smelled it." Keisha sniffed at her pancakes. Right now, she couldn't even think about nasty skunk spray because Grandma Alice had put vanilla in the pancakes, just the way she liked them, and also dusted them with powdered sugar and cinnamon.

"Keisha, eat those before they get cold." Grandma had no patience for picky eaters. "When I was a little girl, you had—"

"Three minutes!" Razi shouted. "Or somebody else got to eat yours."

"Six kids and full-time farmwork. I used to eat dirt for a snack."

Mama gave Grandma a look. The look said, Alice, do not give my boy any more ideas.

"What? Times were hard."

"Was it good?" Razi asked.

Keisha glanced over at baby Paulo, who also chose the Nigerian way. He seemed so happy with ricotta pancakes that he was trying to stuff a whole circle in his mouth.

"Can I get some dirt to try it, Mama? *Please*."

"No." Mama had a way of saying no that nobody questioned. Conversation over.

Using her fork, Keisha popped a small piece of pancake into her mouth. She waited a minute to make sure her mouth was telling her brain the correct information. It was delicious. Very moist and sweet and just a little crispy at the edges.

Alice was watching Keisha with a critical eye. "When are you going to trust your elders, eh, miss? Ricotta cheese comes from a cow just like milk does."

"Mmmmmm," Keisha said.

"Can we go back to the skunk?" Mr. Carter had finished the pancakes on his plate and was eating his dish of fruit. Scoop, scoop, scoop and he was done. Daddy had a lot of stomach to fill.

"I'm not positive there was a skunk, Daddy. The lady said she saw one in her flowers, but skunks don't go out in the daytime. It might have been a cat. So I told him to put out an APB. With the flour."

"Hmmm, yes. An all-paws bulletin. With the flour. Good idea. I wonder if they're leaving food around. . . . That's usually how it starts."

"But why would it spray?" Mama wondered. "Something must have been bothering it."

"Ding-dong," Mr. Sanders said as he came through the door with his twin boys. "We already had our cereal, but maybe we could find room for just one or two pancakes. We need our energy for later on. Big, big day. New member for Wild 4-Ever, I hear. Big ceremony."

Razi smiled. He wiggled a little in his seat. Everyone was looking at him, and that's just how he liked it. "I'm going to say the pledge."

"Mrs. Sanders has promised to make you a special 'no bake' dessert for the occasion. She has weekend college, but the boys and I will be in attendance."

Saturday was Mr. Sanders's regular day off. He delivered the mail for the whole Alger Heights neighborhood and his other day off changed each week, but Saturday he was free all day to be with his two boys, Zeke and Zack. Mr. Carter gave them the nickname the Z-Team. They looked exactly alike except that Zack had a chipped tooth.

Alice pulled another big stack out of the oven and Mama got the chairs from the dining room table. Zeke and Zack took their places between Keisha and Razi and spread napkins on their laps. They were always polite at Mama's table.

Mr. Sanders served himself a single pancake, but Alice put two more on top.

"Alice, you spoil me." There was nothing Mr. Sanders liked better than to come over and eat the Carters' food. Mrs. Sanders was in her second year of the botany program at Grand River Community College, and over the winter she made her kitchen sink into a terrarium. The Z-Team ate a lot of frozen dinners.

"I do have another reason for coming over," Mr. Sanders said, his mouth full of pancake. He held up his finger as he chewed.

"Mmmm. A triumph, Alice. You did it again. How do you make them so fluffy?"

"It's the egg whites," Razi said. "You beat them up and then you fold them in with the cheese."

Zack froze just as his fork was about to enter his mouth. "What cheese?" Zack didn't like cheese, especially the yellow kind.

"No interrupting," Mr. Sanders said. "This is about a murder."

The word "murder" got everyone's attention. They chewed quietly while Mr. Sanders told his story.

"Yesterday, I was finishing up my route when the strangest thing happened. You know that dilapidated brick house at the end of Orchard Street, boys, the one that sits off by itself? An old woman lives there alone—Mrs. Sampson. Mr. Sampson died last year. I still deliver his mail because she might want it.

"Anyway, she doesn't get a lot of personal mail, but there's always third-class stuff, advertisements and catalogs and people asking for money. So yesterday, when I came up the street, a whole flock of crows circled around me as I got near her mailbox. When I went to open the box, they started diving at me! I had to back away. I was afraid I'd lose my balance and spill my mail in the middle of the street!"

"And that's when you got murdered?" Razi asked, his mouth hanging open, full of half-chewed pancake.

"Hush," Mama said, leaning over and tapping the

bottom of Razi's chin. "Or was it a murder of crows, Mr. Sanders?"

"A murder of crows, kids, is what they call a whole group. Strange name. Just like they say a flock of sheep or a gaggle of geese or a parliament of owls."

"Was it a whole flock?" Daddy asked Mr. Sanders. "Or was it a pair? Do you think they were trying to attack you or were they swooping down around you?"

"When something tumbles out of the sky, it's hard to pay attention to details," Mr. Sanders said, patting his hair as if it had just happened.

"It was a murder of crows," Zeke blurted out, reaching for another pancake, even though his mouth was also still full. Zeke was like Daddy and Mr. Sanders. They had a lot of empty spaces to fill.

"I think we should go get 'em," Zack replied. "I'll show those crows they can't do that to my dad!"

"Mr. Zack, concentrate on your breakfast and leave the crow-catching to the professionals." Mama didn't like that sort of talk at her table. When kids started chasing after wild animals, the animals often ended up at Carters' Urban Rescue.

"You have to think like crows. Why would they attack you, Doug? It's not normal behavior," said Daddy.

"Now that I think about it . . . maybe it was

only two," Mr. Sanders said as he eyed the last piece of grilled fruit.

"Have you ever been dive-bombed before?" Daddy picked up the plate. "Would anyone like this last piece of pineapple?"

Keisha knew he was doing it so that Mr. Sanders wouldn't have to ask. She would like it, but guests came first. If only Mr. Sanders didn't have such a large appetite. No one knew where the food went. He was shorter than Daddy but just as skinny. Mama said he walked it all off on his mail route.

"I do!" Razi said. Hopping up and down all the time gave Razi a big appetite, too, though only if something sweet was being offered.

"I will split it between you and Mr. Sanders, then."

"Oh, don't trouble yourself," Mr. Sanders said. But everyone knew he really wanted it. "I'm trying to remember now, about the crows. It was such a surprise. As I got closer to the box, I heard the cawing. I didn't even get to put the mail in. They came at me from two sides and I just ducked my head and ran."

"It's a little-known fact that crows can recognize people," Daddy said. "I read an article about how scientists banded and released crows on a university campus to keep track of them. The crows that had been caught set up quite a racket when those same men and women walked past. You haven't had any run-ins with crows in the past, have you, Doug?"

Mr. Sanders shook his head. "No. Plenty of dogs. A cat or two. Once even a bad-tempered potbellied pig. But no crows."

"Maybe we could go to Mrs. Sampson's after breakfast," Keisha said, "and see if the crows dive on us."

"Yeah! Let's be crow bait!" Zeke said.

"I want to go, too," Razi said. "I want to be crow bait."

Razi didn't even know what crow bait was; he just liked to tag along for everything. Which could get a little annoying when you were the older sister. In fact, one of the reasons she suggested it was so she and Zack and Zeke could ride their bikes around without having to bring Razi.

Not too many parents would let crows swoop down on their children. But the Carters were not like other parents. They understood wild animals better than most and they knew Keisha did, too.

"Well, those crows are either trying to protect something or they're sensing danger," Daddy said. "If it's the first thing, we should figure out what it is so they don't hurt someone else or get hurt themselves. If it's the second thing, we have to figure out what makes your dad so scary."

"Our dad isn't scary," Zack said. "He was the clown in the Hollyhock Parade."

"To crows, I mean." Daddy wiped his face with his napkin and dropped it back on his lap. "If your dad agrees, you three can ride your bikes over to Mrs. Sampson's house. Keisha will know if it's a dangerous situation. And you, Z-Team, will have to let Keisha make the decisions. Can you do that?"

"Sure. We have to listen to her lots of times at school," Zack said.

"What about me?" Razi asked, pushing his plate away.

Grandma Alice put her hand on Razi's arm. "We will stay here and strip the peas and shuck the corn for dinner," she said.

"Awww." Razi started to protest, but he loved taking things apart. From under lowered eyelids, he asked Mama: "Can I keep the silk?"

The last time Razi shucked the corn, there were little strands of corn silk all over the house.

"Yes, but in the back. Not in the house."

"I can give it to Big Bob for the birds. Corn silk is very comfy."

"But will it still be that way next spring?" Keisha began collecting the plates from the table. The Wild 4-Ever Club was gathering warm natural materials like feathers, animal hair and wool to hang out early next spring when birds were looking for soft things to line their nests.

"I'm making a silk present for Big Bob."

Why argue with Razi? When he got an idea into his head, it stuck like a bur. Everybody liked their club leader, Big Bob. For thirty years, he was a biology teacher at Grand River Community College. He had a full beard that was red where it wasn't white and lots of muscles for an old guy. Now he had time for what he called his encore career as a veterinary tech at the Humane Society. Big Bob cared for animals, too. Only he cared for the kinds of animals that people kept as pets—puppies, kittens, bunnies . . . puppies.

Keisha reached for the kitchen towel to help Mama with the dishes, but Mama shooed her away.

"Mr. Sanders and I can do this. He's very good at wiping dishes. You go ahead, Ada. I want you back in time to practice the pledge with Razi before his big ceremony."

Keisha nodded. When Mama called her by her pet name, Ada—which, in the Igbo language, meant the first daughter—Keisha knew Mama was asking her to act like an adult.

Mama leaned down and kissed her forehead. "But be careful. Crows are powerful."

Chapter 2

What was it about the Z-Team that made them always need to ride up front? Ever since they got their trick bikes, Zack and Zeke rode side by side. When there was a speed bump, they flew over it together and gave each other a high five. Zack and Zeke got along best when they were on their bikes.

Late summer was Keisha's favorite time of year. She rode behind the Z-Team, taking in the tall sycamore trees that spread their branches up and over the street. It felt like riding through a leafy green tunnel. Now that it was August, Mrs. Paretsky dressed the plastic goose on her front step in a polka-dot dress with a little scarf tied on its head. Her grandchildren made dandelion necklaces for the goose to wear.

Zack called back to Keisha something about Jorge. They were close to Jorge's house and riding at top speed. Keisha wasn't even sure she'd heard him right. Jorge knew a lot about birds, but Mama and Daddy hadn't said it was okay to bring Jorge.

"Let's go by ourselves first!" she called out to them.

Zack put his hand to his ear. "Can't hear you," he shouted back.

It didn't help that they were riding past the alley behind Eleanor Street and all the kids outside were screaming. That meant the Vanderests had turned the sprinkler on. Even though they were old, the Vanderests loved children. In the summer, Mrs. Vanderest brought out paint and let anyone who wanted to paint the rocks that lined the street in their front yard. She never said that the rocks had to wear red, white and blue colors for the Hollyhock Parade, but they always did. And when you had to rest from pedaling your heavy decorated bicycle, you could sit on the big rocks and get some Hoggy Doggy Double Dutch Chocolate ice cream. Every little container had a wooden paddle to scoop out the ice cream. There was always enough, even when some kids took two.

Now the Z-Team cut down the alley, making the little ones scream even more as they splashed in the puddles from the sprinkler.

"Jorge!" they shouted up to Jorge's second-floor apartment, two doors down from the Vanderests' house.

"Hey." Jorge stepped out onto the second-floor porch. He had baby Carmelo in his arms. "Where do you think you're going without me?"

Jorge lived with his grandparents. Jorge was the Z-Team's best friend. Sometimes he got along better with Zack, sometimes Zeke. Sometimes the twins fought over Jorge, which made him feel special because Jorge was an only child.

"We were just coming to get you," Zack said, his bike skidding to a stop. "Get on. We got to go talk to some crows."

"Let me ask." Jorge disappeared from view.

"Hello? Who decided this?" Keisha asked the Z-Team as she caught up. "We might get in trouble."

"I asked you just now," Zack said. "When we were riding."

"Didn't you hear him?" Zeke asked.

"What I said was—"

"I was pretty sure you said yes."

Jorge opened the front door and Zack jumped to the ground so his friend could climb on back.

If it were anyone other than Jorge, Keisha would have told him to stay home. But Jorge was good with animals, too. He was especially good with birds.

When things got boring on the playground, Jorge would do birdcalls for the kids. All they had to do was point at a bird and he could make the noise. Sparrow, robin, pigeon, crow. Didn't matter. He could do other birds, too, even if they didn't come around the playground. That's because Big Bob had showed Jorge how to look up birdcalls on the Internet one evening after a Wild 4-Ever Club meeting.

Keisha knew a lot about birds and she tried to learn to make their calls, but nobody was as good as Jorge.

"Hi, Keisha," Jorge said. "I have to be back in an hour to take care of Carmelo so Wita can go shopping." Carmelo was Jorge's baby cousin and Wita was Jorge's name for his grandma. When he was little, he couldn't pronounce the whole word in Spanish—"*abuelita*"—so he said "wita" and it stuck.

"Are you bringing Carmelo to the Wild 4-Ever Club meeting tonight?"

Jorge nodded. "Wita has to work."

Keisha was glad that Carmelo was coming. Carmelo and Paulo were baby friends.

Jorge didn't have a bike, so he always stood on the pegs at the back of one of the Z-Team's bikes.

"Ride with me, Jorge," Zeke said.

Keisha thought there would be a long discussion: "No, me." "No! Me!"

But there wasn't. The twins must really want to see these crows. Zack hopped back on his bike. Jorge stepped on the pegs of Zeke's bike and grabbed his shoulders.

"I'll tell you about the murder while we ride," Zack shouted as they took off.

Soon they were in a part of Alger Heights that Keisha didn't know very well. It was close to Burton

Street, a very busy four-lane street. Mama didn't like Keisha to ride her bike there. But Mr. Sanders let Zack and Zeke ride anywhere on his mail route, so they knew where they were going. They turned down a road that had bigger houses than most of the ones her friends lived in. They were older, too—brick houses with gates out front and painted-black iron railings and bars over the windows. The people who lived in those houses weren't as friendly as Mrs. Paretsky or the Vanderests.

Zack and Zeke were talking to each other and pointing. They sped up and turned in between two brick pillars that marked the entrance to a street called Orchard Court. There was a big house at the far end.

They rode ahead of Keisha, straight toward the house.

Too late, Keisha saw the crows circling overhead.

"Run for your life!" Zack shouted as a crow swooped toward him. Jorge jumped off as Zeke dropped his bike to the ground and ran. Keisha slowed up, trying to figure out what the crow was protecting. As she got closer to the driveway, she saw the mailbox. Another crow dove down, screeching. This one came from behind her. Others were in the trees above, hopping up and down and cawing. Full-sized crows were big! Like a football with wings and claws! Swish! Swoop!

There was nothing to do but drop her bike and run, too.

"Keisha, quick!" The boys had found a trellis covered with vines and were taking cover beneath it. "It's an attack. Hide over here!"

As soon as Keisha left the area near the mailbox, the crows retreated to the trees. They kept making noise, though. Caw! Caw! Craw! A crow racket could wake the whole neighborhood.

"They're awful mad about something," Zeke said.

"What do you think, Jorge?" Keisha had to redo her ponytail after the ride and getting swooped by crows.

She tucked all the pieces that had sprung out back under her headband.

Jorge didn't answer. He was watching the crows.

"It's like we were attacking them just by riding our bikes," Zack said, panting.

"Yeah. What did we do?" Zeke wondered.

Now that the crows were settling, Keisha had a chance to look around and think about it. They had been coming down the street toward the big brick house at the end, but as soon as they got near the mailbox, the crows went crazy.

Keisha looked up at the house. The wood was sagging on the front porch, and Keisha could see little gaps between the stones in the foundation. She watched as a chipmunk darted into the downspout and popped up on the roof in a spot where the spout had come apart.

That was when she saw an old woman's face in the second-floor window. It startled Keisha. Was the woman watching them?

"Hey, Jorge, what are they saying?" Zack asked.

"They sound mad," Jorge said, his eyes scanning the trees, "but crows don't get mad for no reason. I think they're trying to protect something. Something in the mailbox."

"In the mailbox? Do you think they're waiting for a package?" Zack laughed and pulled a few purplish green grapes off a bunch by his side. He rolled them around in his fingers until the skins started to split.

"*Don't pick those,*" Keisha warned Zack. "There's an old lady in that house watching us."

A strange sound came from inside the mailbox. It sounded a little like a stick scratching on metal. The mailbox door was open just a crack.

"Did you see that?" Zack said. He had the best eyes of the four. "A head just popped out of the mailbox."

"Did not," said Zeke.

"Did so," said Zack.

"*That,*" said Jorge, "is what the crows are protecting."

Keisha nodded. "It's the right time of year for crow nestlings," she said.

"But how did it get in the mailbox?" Zeke wanted to know.

"More important—" Keisha stopped talking and started thinking like a wildlife rehabilitator. "How long has it been in there? And how are we going to get it out?"

"You kids get away from those grapes!" The children turned to see the old lady coming out of her house, swinging a broom. "I'm serious. This is private property."

Jorge ducked behind Zack, who put his hands

behind his back and looked at the ground. Zeke pushed Keisha forward. She was the one who knew how to talk to old ladies.

"Stay here," Keisha ordered the boys. "And don't even touch those grapes."

"I'm Keisha Carter," she said when she got to the bottom of the porch steps. "My mom and dad run Carters' Urban Rescue. We were riding our bikes and, well, I think you have a baby bird in your mailbox."

"Of course I have a baby bird in my mailbox. I put it there myself."

"Why would you put a baby crow in your mailbox?"

"To save it from the cat, of course."

"Has it been in there long?"

"Three hours and twenty-seven minutes. The cat just left."

"But how will it eat?"

"Well, it's been fluttering around my mailbox since yesterday, and so I scattered some seed around. . . . Now I've put some seeds in the mailbox, too. And a bowl of water. That was no easy task with crows all over me."

"But they don't eat seeds," Keisha said. "Not the babies . . . and you have to give them water from a syringe."

"What's your name again?" The woman looked Keisha up and down, trying to decide if she believed a

ten-year-old girl was capable of knowing how baby crows drink.

But before Keisha could answer, she added: "And

where did your friends learn their manners? I make grape juice for God's Kitchen with those grapes."

Keisha couldn't wait to tell the boys they'd been squishing God's grapes!

"The thing is, Mrs. Sampson, it's getting hot in that mailbox even in the shade. That baby crow will get dehydrated and that could kill it."

"How do you know my name? Have you been snooping?" Mrs. Sampson leaned on her broom. She looked tired.

"Mr. Sanders told us. He's your postman. And their dad." Keisha waved at the boys and smiled big, hoping they would return a cheerful wave, which they did.

"Mr. Snoopers is more like it. What business is it of his to tell those grape-plucking hooligans my name?"

"About this baby crow . . ." Keisha pulled the family business card out of her pocket. "I think maybe my dad can help."

Mrs. Sampson squinted at the business card. "Are you trying to sell me something, young lady? Because, if so, I need to have everything in writing. People take advantage of the elderly, you know."

Keisha sighed. While she was trying to explain things to Mrs. Sampson, that little bird was getting more and more dehydrated.

"I know. I'll bring my dad back here and you can

talk to him." She left Mrs. Sampson waving her finger and rushed back to the boys.

"Hurry up, guys," she called out to them, pulling her bike out of the tangle. "As soon as we drop Jorge off, we've got a baby crow to rescue."

Chapter 3

Keisha and the Z-Team rode their bikes into the yard so fast they almost got into a pileup with Daddy's Havahart traps. Wen and Aaliyah stood in the driveway with their beaded, red, white and blue double-Dutch jump ropes, watching the commotion.

"We need a crossing guard in this driveway," Aaliyah said, "to make sure there are no accidents."

"No, we need to save a baby bird!" Zack cried, dropping his bike on the ground. "All hands on deck."

"What does that mean?" Zeke asked, putting his bike up against Daddy's truck.

"It means we all have to get ready."

"What are you talking about?" Aaliyah said. "It's time to practice."

"Not yet, Aaliyah." Keisha looked around for Daddy. "Where is everybody?"

"Your mama took Razi and Paulo to the children's museum," Wen said. "And your dad's going to drive us to the Mount Zion Church parking lot so we can practice double Dutch in the shade."

Daddy came to the door, jingling the truck keys

and whistling. "I want to stop at the hardware store while you girls are jumping," he said. "Oh, boys, your mother called and asked me to send you home. You've got to mow the lawn."

"Awww, we just gave the grass a haircut." Zeke got back on his bike and turned it around.

"Can't we wait until after we see the murder again?" Zack asked.

"See the murder *again?*" Aaliyah dropped her jump rope on the ground. "I never understand what is going on around here."

"How did it go at Mrs. Sampson's house?"

Keisha told everyone about the baby crow in the mailbox. "A murder is a group of crows, Aaliyah. It's not a real murder."

Zack untangled his bicycle from the traps. "You don't have to tell her everything, Keisha. Now we can't brag about seeing a real murder."

"But we did see a real murder." Zeke took off down the driveway. "I get the front yard," he called back over his shoulder.

"Do not! I did the back last time."

"Did not!"

The girls watched them go, the Z-team repeating "did not" all the way down the street.

Daddy scratched the side of his face. "Hmmm.

Maybe we better go there first. Keisha, put together a baby bird first-aid kit, would you?"

"Can Aaliyah and Wen come with us to see the baby crow?" Keisha asked.

"Aaliyah will have to call Moms."

Aaliyah was already coiling up the rope. She pulled out her cell phone. "Just don't make me go near crows. I like crows to stay where they live—in the trees—and me to stay on the sidewalk. If Moms knew I was messin' with crows, she wouldn't let me play with Keisha anymore."

Wen grabbed Keisha's hand and they had an eye giggle together. That's where you laugh about something, but you don't let the laugh spread to your whole face. Aaliyah spent her summers with her grandma—who everybody called Moms—while her parents worked. Unlike Wen's parents, Moms needed to be called whenever the plans changed. Aaliyah was always telling the girls that her Moms would never let her do this or that, but Keisha and Wen thought Moms was nice. She braided Keisha's hair and made the best "sweet tea" north of Montgomery, Alabama. That's where her people were from.

Grandma showed up on the front steps dragging the beach umbrella. "I heard, I heard," she said. "I call the front seat."

"But we're not going to be in the sun."

"Oh, great balls of Fiorenza, I've got my reasons."

The girls knew it was useless to argue with Grandma, so they put their ropes and her beach umbrella in the back of the truck.

"Okay, a baby bird kit . . ." Keisha started to count off on her fingers. "One, there's a cardboard shoe box and a bag of shredded paper by the recycling pile in the garage. Aaliyah can find that. Hmmm. Two, Wen, a bottle of filtered water and a syringe from the shed in the back where we keep the animal supplies."

Wen and Aaliyah had done this before. They knew where everything was. Keisha headed to the office.

"Don't forget the eggshells," Grandma called from the truck. "Baby crows need their calcium."

"Yup." Keisha ran to the office desk and pulled out the bird file, flipping through it until she found the section on crows. Baby birds need very different food. They aren't like puppies, for instance. Puppies all eat pretty much the same thing.

Mama said puppies were always on Keisha's mind. She said Keisha was a puppy magnet. If there was a picture of a puppy in the newspaper or a commercial on TV with a puppy or even a puppy hanging out the window of the car next to them, letting its adorable little tongue taste the breeze, Keisha would see it and call it out for everyone else to see.

But as she scanned the fact sheet about baby crows, Keisha knew there was another reason to be thinking about puppies, and that was because one of the things baby crows like to eat was mashed-up puppy food.

She ran down to the basement and took a handful of puppy chow out of the bin by the freezer. She also grabbed a little plastic bag of frozen crickets. Back upstairs, she got a hard-boiled egg from the fridge. She put two crickets, a quarter cup of water and the puppy chow in the microwave for ninety seconds. Then she sliced the whole egg in half, scooped out the yolk and crackled up the shell. She dumped everything in the animals' food processor and whirled it around. Yum. Crow food! She dumped it all into a plastic tub and stuck on the lid.

Daddy was warming up the truck. Grandma was in the front, and Wen and Aaliyah were in the back in ABC order. Aaliyah always called ABC order so she could sit by a window.

She handed the shoe box full of shredded paper to Keisha, who used her fist to make a well in the center, kind of like a nest.

"It doesn't seem very soft," Wen said. "Cotton balls would be nicer, don't you think?"

"Don't you remember from our last Wild 4-Ever meeting?" Aaliyah said. "Big Bob said you can't use anything that gets caught in their feet. Cotton balls and crow talons are not a good mix."

"That's good recall, Aaliyah," Daddy said. "And it's true, too."

Aaliyah patted her braids. She liked it when Daddy said nice things about her memory. "They make messy nests, too. Remember the—"

"I need your eyes, ladies," Daddy interrupted.

"Look for the big brick posts," Keisha said. "That's where you turn in."

Aaliyah grabbed Keisha's knee. "Wen wants to do freestyle, but I think we should do double unders. What do you think, Keisha?"

"Explain them again," Daddy said. He could never keep it straight.

"Oh, for heaven's sake," Grandma sighed. "It's not that complicated."

When Keisha was little, Grandma was a jump rope judge. But now that Keisha was competing, Grandma couldn't concentrate on judging anyone else, so she became the oldest Langston Hughes Steppers cheerleader. She even had a megaphone.

"There are four forms, and all have equal weight in judging," Grandma told Daddy. "One-minute speed jumping, three-minute speed jumping, double unders and freestyle."

"'Double unders' means the rope goes underneath your feet twice, right?" Daddy asked.

"Yup."

"Mr. Rose said that with Aaliyah coming up this year, he's thinking about entering the Langston Hughes Steppers in the triple-under competition." Wen patted Aaliyah's leg. Aaliyah was the only one in the school who could do a whole minute of triple unders.

"Oops. Sorry, Daddy. That's where you turn. . . . See that big brick post?"

"Hold on!" Daddy turned the wheel sharp, and the jar of baby crow food bounced from Keisha's lap to Wen's. Wen held it up. "Looks like miso paste," she said.

"Do you eat miso paste?" Keisha asked.

"We make soup with it," Wen said.

Whatever miso paste was, Keisha was in no hurry to try it.

Daddy parked in the driveway.

"Hey, I know this house," Aaliyah said. "She's at the community center sometimes. Moms brought her some soup. We could practice in this driveway." Aaliyah hopped out of the truck and ran down the driveway.

"Aaliyah, no!" Keisha was too late. Aaliyah ran right near the mailbox. The crows in the trees hub-bub-bubbed, as Razi would say, cawing loudly to each other. Two crows dove down toward Aaliyah.

Aaliyah covered her head and ducked. "Birds, don't mess with my braids!" She ran bent over back to the truck.

"You silly girl. That's what the umbrella's for!" Grandma shouted out the window.

"For cover," Daddy said. "Mom, what a splendid idea."

"Well, if we'd had a CFC, I would have told you." Grandma liked it best when she got to go over plans beforehand at a Carter Family Conference.

"Is that Mrs. Sampson?" Wen asked, pointing to the lady in the window.

Keisha nodded. Mrs. Sampson was in her same spot by the second-floor window. How much time does she spend there? Keisha wondered.

Daddy got out of the truck and went to the front door. Keisha followed him.

"Unplug me, Wen," Grandma said. Wen jumped out of the truck.

"They got their little crow toenails in my swirl!" Aaliyah said, patting the top of her head. "Moms is gonna die."

"It looks fine," Wen said, helping Grandma with the seat belt. "They didn't get that close."

"I felt their hot crow breath. It was like sour cherries."

"Where's your crown, drama queen?" Grandma said, laughing as she scooched herself over to the open door, grabbed Wen's hand and stepped out of the truck.

Daddy knocked on the door and called out: "Carters' Urban Rescue! Here about a baby crow."

Mrs. Sampson opened the door. "I'm old, but I'm not deaf."

Grandma came up the walk. "It's me," she said. "I'm the deaf one. He can't adjust. Alice Carter." She took Mrs. Sampson's wrinkled hand in her own.

Daddy pulled out the family card that read, WHATEVER THE DILEMMA, IF IT'S GOT FUR OR FEATHERS, THE CARTERS ARE THE ONES TO CALL! 555-7803.

"I understand you have a baby crow in the mailbox," Daddy said.

Mrs. Sampson nodded. "There was a cat. I don't move that fast. The mailbox was the first thing I came to."

"This baby needs help, Mrs. Sampson. If he stays in your mailbox much longer, he'll likely starve. We feed our baby crows every twenty minutes."

"Oh dear. I put some seeds in the box, but now I can't get near it."

"Crow-diving is hard for the balance," Grandma agreed.

"But we do have a rescue plan." Daddy glanced back at the truck, where Aaliyah was shaking her head no. "I have three strong girls here. You've met my daughter, Keisha. And this is our friend Wen.

"They will transport a beach umbrella to the mailbox and I will transfer the baby to this temporary nest." He held out the shoe box filled with shredded paper.

"Then we can either drive him back to our place, or . . ." Daddy craned his long neck to see into Mrs. Sampson's house. "We could examine him right here and begin treatment immediately."

Mrs. Sampson turned her head to follow Daddy's gaze. "I wasn't expecting company."

"Just a few minutes at your kitchen table will do the trick."

"I suppose . . . Better use the dining room table. There's more light in there."

"Excellent." Daddy seized the moment. "Keisha, Wen, get the umbrella. Mom, why don't you stay here on the porch with Mrs. Sampson? There might be jostling and I notice you didn't bring your cane."

"I can walk just fine without it."

"Maybe so, but you promised to have it with you on all rescue operations."

"But it's so OL," Grandma complained. "OL" meant "Old Lady." Grandma didn't like anything that made her seem old.

"Not the pink one," Wen said. Wen loved pink.

There are beach umbrellas and there are beach umbrellas. Some make only enough shade to cover your towel for an hour before you have to move it to keep off the sun. But others, like Grandma Alice's, are big enough to shade a family of six at Millennium Park for most of the day. Daddy said that Razi should never hold on to that umbrella in a breeze or it would lift him right up into the clouds.

Keisha jumped into the back of the truck. Putting

her hands around the big folds of fabric, she hoisted the umbrella over the lip of the truck bed. Wen took it by the handle and stood it up. Together, the girls unfastened the umbrella and cranked it open.

"Whoa!" Keisha grabbed it as high up as she could reach; Wen held on to the middle by the crank. But still, the umbrella teetered.

Daddy rushed over. "Okay, ladies, ready for Operation Baby Crow Rescue?"

"Ready," the girls said together.

"On the count of three, I'll grab up here and we'll all walk together." Daddy only had one hand free because he had to hold the box with the nest in his other hand.

Already the big crows were bouncing on the branches above and cawing like crazy, even though the rescuers weren't close to the mailbox yet.

"This is worse than the Langston Hughes auditorium during a free-throw shoot in overtime." Aaliyah had rolled down the window and stuck her head out.

"Once we get close in, they're going to dive-bomb us, ladies, so be prepared."

"What does that mean?" Wen asked. She was ducking already.

"Like what happened a minute ago," Keisha said, "only they'll hit the umbrella and not the top of your head. Just hold tight."

"One, two . . . three!"

They set off. At first, the bottom of the umbrella got going faster than the top, and that made it tip to the left. Then the girls pulled it in the other direction and it went too far to the right.

"Maybe if we do a chant, we can find our rhythm," Keisha shouted over the sound of unhappy crows.

"Good idea." Wen began: "I like coffee, I like tea. I want Keisha to jump with me."

"I like coffee, I like tea. I want Wen to jump with me," Aaliyah shouted from the truck.

It worked! They were moving.

Just when Daddy was saying, "Almost there, girls . . ."

Boom! Poom!

It felt like Marcus, the star basketball player at their school, had landed a double pump right on top of the umbrella.

"Watch out!" Aaliyah screamed.

"Whoa!" Wen stumbled.

"Hold on, girls," Daddy said, leaning down toward the mailbox. "We've got an incoming crow mama and daddy!"

Chapter 4

"Don't be afraid, Wen. The crows are just trying to protect their baby," Keisha said, struggling to keep the umbrella straight up. "Don't pull us over, Daddy!"

Daddy had bent over to open the mailbox and taken his end of the umbrella with him. He let go now so he could use his free hand to pull the little crow out by its feet.

Poom! Poom!

"Hold tight, Wen, we're almost there." Keisha could see how weak and frightened the little bird was because it kept its head turned away and its feet up and didn't even try to defend itself.

"Okay, girls, let's beat a retreat."

As they moved away from the mailbox, the diving crows stopped just as suddenly as they had started. Keisha wondered if they thought their baby was still in the mailbox. If so, Carters' Urban Rescue hadn't solved Mr. Sanders's problem.

"On the count of three," Daddy said when they reached the front walk, "drop the umbrella and run. One, two, three . . ."

The girls dropped the umbrella and ran. Grandma

held the door open until they got through it and into the dark hallway. They were panting by the time they reached Mrs. Sampson's dining room table. Sometime during the rescue operation, Aaliyah had scooted from the truck into Mrs. Sampson's house. Now she was examining the top of her head in Mrs. Sampson's front hall mirror.

"Well, I've never seen such a crow-motion," Grandma said, slamming the door. "Here, use my sweater, Fred."

Daddy spread Grandma's sweater on the table and laid the baby crow on top of it. "Please step back, everyone . . . all but Keisha. I need a little help examining the patient."

Aaliyah, Wen and Grandma were familiar with this part of animal rescuing, too. They knew how stressful these situations were for the birds and the other animals, and so they stepped back and stayed quiet.

"I was an army nurse," Mrs. Sampson said, standing behind a dining room chair and turning off the overhead light. There was plenty of light coming through the window. The baby crow was as big as a twenty-ounce soda bottle, with eyes the color of the blue rock candy they bought at Charley's candy store.

Daddy took hold of the crow's head. Cradling it in his fingers so the crow couldn't bite him, he turned the little head back and forth. Keisha watched closely.

"It doesn't look like a baby," Aaliyah whispered as Daddy pressed his fingers along each wing to check for injuries.

"Crows grow quickly, Aaliyah. When a bird this big can't fly, people think it's injured, even though it may just be young."

The little crow opened its mouth and gave a baby-crow-sized caw.

"You're hurting it, Fred," Grandma whispered.

"No, Mom. I think that's a good sign. He's scared, but he's hungry."

Even though the Carter rescue team had stepped back, Mrs. Sampson leaned forward to examine the patient. Keisha noticed her nose was very close to the crow's beak.

"I served as a nurse in the Sixty-eighth Women's Army Corps, arriving 1943, in Cairo, Egypt. I was stationed at the medevac hospital there." She leaned back and polished her glasses. "There's nothing wrong with this crow that a competent nurse can't fix."

"You may be right, Mrs. Sampson. Keisha, can I get some help?" Daddy took the crow in one hand and put out his palm. Keisha removed the lid of the Tupperware container. The strong smell of egg/cricket/puppy chow that had sat in a hot truck filled the room.

"That's quite an odor," Mrs. Sampson remarked.

Keisha noticed Aaliyah was plugging her nose.

"Maybe it smells good to a crow," Wen suggested.

"Crows don't have a sense of smell," Daddy added. "When you think about it, that probably comes in handy with some of the things they eat."

"Don't tell us any more until after lunch, Mr. Carter," Aaliyah pleaded. "I'm begging you. . . ."

Daddy nodded to Keisha, who began making pea-sized lumps out of the food in the container. She lined them up on the edge of the table. "Aaliyah, will you get a glass of water to fill this syringe?"

"I have some distilled water in the fridge," Mrs. Sampson said. "That would be more hygienic."

"That's even better than our filtered water. I'll get it. Which way is the kitchen?"

Mrs. Sampson pointed, and Grandma disappeared down the hall. As Keisha watched her go, she noticed the clothes draped over the chairs and the old newspapers piled up in the corner. All these things meant that Mrs. Sampson's home was not in tip-top shape, something the Carters had to make their home every Sunday morning before church. Mrs. Sampson's house probably hadn't been tip-top for some time.

Daddy shifted the little crow so he could hold up its head while keeping its wings pinned to its body. "I pronounce this crow healthy . . . and hungry. Keisha?"

Keisha had a lot of experience feeding baby birds and her fingers were smaller than Daddy's, so she usually got the job of stuffing the bird food mush down the birds' throats. Then, after the birds weren't so frightened, Keisha or Daddy could use the syringe to get some water in them.

She pressed one of the blobs of food onto her pointer finger and waved it near the crow's eye. As she moved her finger, the little crow became very interested. Suddenly he tilted his  head back and opened his beak wide. Keisha quickly stuck the plug of food deep in his throat.

"Goodness," Mrs. Sampson said. "You'll choke the poor thing."

"That's how the mama does it," Daddy said. "When you get that far down, it stimulates the little guy to swallow."

"What if he bites you, Keisha?" Aaliyah asked.

"It doesn't hurt that much," Daddy told Aaliyah. "Plus, he wants this food, just like baby Paulo."

"And the crow doesn't have teeth," Keisha said, remembering how much it hurt to get her fingers near Paulo's mouth when he was teething.

Wen started to ask a question, but she was inter-rupted by the crow's squawking.

"What does *that* mean?" Aaliyah asked. "He's not happy."

Daddy stroked the feathers at the little crow's throat. "It sounds bad, but it means he feels good, Aaliyah. Loosely translated, he's saying, 'Yum. Keep it coming.'"

Keisha got into a rhythm with the little crow that sounded like "squawk, shlump, glump." When he started to slow down, Daddy added a few drops of water with the syringe in between plugs of food.

After a time, the crow closed his mouth and turned his head away. Daddy set him in his nest box, which he then set inside a larger box they'd brought along. Quick as a wink, he took a dish towel that had been sitting over the back of the chair and tossed it over the box.

"We don't want to encourage that," he said as he smoothed the material over the sides.

"What? Encourage what?" Aaliyah had just stepped in closer to get a better look.

"Now that he's fed and feels a little safer, he'll be looking around. And it's possible he could imprint on one of us."

"Ew." Aaliyah crossed her arms. "You mean, like, on our clothes?"

"No, Aaliyah. 'Imprint' means he could think that we're, well, like his mama or his daddy or his . . . Moms." Daddy set the crow's box on a chair, which he then pushed to face the wall. He turned back to Mrs. Sampson.

"Now I need to figure out where we're going to put the little guy while he's building up his strength. We just filled up our bird enclosure with ducklings."

"I'm confused." Mrs. Sampson sat down at the table and looked around as if the thought had just occurred to her: *Where did you all come from?* "Don't babies stay in the nest until they're ready to fly?"

"No," Daddy and Grandma said together. They were used to this question.

"When people see a crow this big that can't fly, they think there must be something wrong with it," Daddy said. "So here are the signs to look for. (1) Is it bleeding? (2) Is it dragging a wing? (3) Is it in immediate danger? You responded to number three. You rescued the baby crow from the cat."

"But if it can't fly, won't it be in danger until it can?"

"Yes, but it can't learn to fly until it goes through the fledgling phase. Now, let me explain just a few things about crow biology—"

Grandma Alice smacked her hands on the table. "I'm parched," she said. "Can I get myself a glass of water?"

"Of course," Mrs. Sampson said. "There's a jelly jar in the cupboard over the sink. That's what I use."

"Anybody else want water?"

"Yes. Thank you, Mom."

Aaliyah stood at the window. "The court is far enough away from the mailbox. . . . We could still get a little practice in. . . ."

Like Grandma, Aaliyah didn't enjoy listening to Daddy's educational speeches. In fact, the only person who did seem interested was Mrs. Sampson. Wen tugged on Keisha's shorts and nodded toward the window.

"Baby birds have many natural predators. Cats . . . hawks, of course, and raccoons and snakes, who also go after the eggs."

Grandma came back into the room and put jelly jars of water in front of her son and Mrs. Sampson. She stood there looking at her son, her hands on her hips.

"So, a wild cat will search for food night after night. Eventually, it will find a nest. But if the birds are moving around like this little guy here, there is a much better chance for survival. And yet, you have to take into account—"

"Oh my goodness, look at the time," Grandma interrupted Daddy. "We've still got to go see about a skunk!"

Daddy looked around, surprised. "Is it that late?" He glanced at his watch. "Well, I guess it is."

"Funny how time flies even when the crows don't," Grandma replied, heading for the door. The girls followed after her.

Outside, they climbed into the backseat, and Keisha watched out the window. It was a few minutes before Daddy said good-bye to Mrs. Sampson. "Where's the crow?" she asked as Daddy got in the cab.

He turned the key in the ignition and the engine rattled a few seconds before starting up. "Sometimes you have to explore the gray area."

"What's the gray area?" Wen wanted to know.

"The gray area was in her cupboard," Grandma said. "Stale crackers and miller moths everywhere. And her milk was past the sell-by date."

"Maybe that's why she seemed so tired." Keisha stared out the window, wondering how one little old lady could keep a big house like that in order.

Daddy adjusted the rearview mirror so he could see Wen. "The gray area is not right and not wrong . . . not black and not white. Mrs. Sampson used to be a nurse, and now she has learned how to nurse a crow. It will be less stressful for the crow if he can stay at her house and not have to move in with a bunch of ducklings."

"So why is that gray?" Aaliyah asked. "Why isn't it right?"

"Long story," Grandma replied.

Keisha knew what was wrong about it. Mrs. Sampson was not a licensed wildlife rehabilitator. Officially it was against the law for her to take care of the little crow. People did it all the time and they often did it wrong, so the law was made to protect animals from being mistreated, even by accident, and to protect people from possibly getting hurt by caring for dangerous wild animals.

Keisha waited until they had dropped off Aaliyah and Wen before asking Daddy more about the gray area.

"I know that technically it's not right, but we don't have the staff for all these cases, Key. Since she used to be a nurse, Mrs. Sampson can help us out on this one. And it's good for older people to have some purpose. This one time is okay." Daddy turned into the alley behind their house.

"It won't take long, will it?" Keisha asked.

"My guess is two to three days and he'll be ready to try the great outdoors again. I just want to keep the little guy quiet, get some protein in him and make sure he's hydrated. I think I'll wait on the hardware store for now. Might be time for a little R&R in the CFH." Daddy whistled a little tune to himself. Thinking about rest and relaxation in the Carter family hammock always made Daddy happy.

As the truck pulled to a stop in their driveway, Keisha wondered what would make Mrs. Sampson happy enough to whistle.

Chapter 5

"Oh, no, you don't, Mr. Carter," Mama said, handing Paulo to Daddy just as he was heading for the hammock. "Sticky babies are your responsibility."

Razi took the baby from Daddy and held him up. "Paulo doesn't want Daddy! Paulo votes for me!" Razi blew raspberries on Paulo's stomach until he giggled. "See?"

Grandma Alice wanted her turn with baby Paulo. She held out her arms. "You know as well as I do, Razi Carter, that your daddy is the best one in the family for bathing babies."

Grandma looked Razi up and down. "I must say you look fine in your dress shirt."

"Mama says I can wear the clip-on tie, like I do at church." Razi twisted his fingers together. "But not until we get to the center. Grandma, you put it in your purse."

Grandma checked her watch. "You're ready for the ceremony, but we've still got an hour to go." She looked at Mama, then at Daddy. "Can we swirl him in plastic wrap until it's time?"

"I tried to get him to wait." Mama fingered Razi's

hair and rubbed behind his ears. "He wanted to get dressed an hour ago."

"Well, speaking of stomachs," Grandma said, tickling Paulo's tummy. "We've got laundry to fold, animal pens to clean, a baby to bathe and tummies to fill, though we can't call it lunch. It's too late for that. Maybe *linner* or *dunch*. And if anyone's going to get some R&R, it's going to be me. I have to rest my beauty, after all."

"Dunch!" Razi said. "I vote for dunch!"

"I will get the dunch," Mama said.

"I'll take the laundry off the line," Keisha offered.

"And *we*, my friend," Daddy said to the baby as he took Paulo from Grandma, "have a date with some soap bubbles and a tub filled with water. And because your older brother is an almost-official member of Wild 4-Ever, I am going to let him be my bath master apprentice today."

Daddy loved bath time because he liked making up stories and he always said bath time was the best time for imagining.

Paulo, who didn't mind being fed by anyone who was available, would sit in the tub with a little frown on his face and his fists closed tight if Mama or Keisha ran the bathwater. For some reason, Daddy got in a habit of wearing a fake mustache while he started the bathwater. Then he would give an elaborate sneeze and the mustache would stick to the wet tile. Paulo laughed and laughed.

"What does an 'apprentice' mean, Daddy?" Razi asked, jumping up and down and tugging on Daddy's T-shirt. "What does an apprentice do?"

"It's the junior version of something."

"It's settled." Grandma planted a kiss on Paulo's head. "Just don't let Razi immerse himself in his field of study, Fred. I ironed that shirt."

And then—snip, snap, clip clap, as Grandma Alice liked to say—it was time for Grandma, Razi and Keisha to hold hands and walk to the Baxter Community Center for the Wild 4-Ever Club meeting. Mama and Daddy would wait for Mr. Sanders and wheel Paulo over in the stroller. Then they would sit in the back and be the *proud* parents, Mama told Razi.

"When will Mama and Daddy come? What if the baby cries?" Razi asked as they walked. He was getting all his worrying done ahead of time.

"Carmelo's coming," Keisha told him, "so they won't cry. They will goo-goo and ga-ga at each other."

"It's easy to have fun when you're a baby," Razi said. "Keisha, will you say the pledge with me?"

Grandma, Razi and Keisha stopped for the light at James Street. Keisha waited until they had crossed to say, "You know it, Razi! I know you do. Tell it to me right now."

Razi took a big breath. He stopped walking. He put his hand over his heart. "I pledge my head to clearer thinking, my heart to greater loyal—"

Grandma elbowed Keisha. "Don't mouth the words," she whispered. "It's so amateur." Keisha had practiced with Razi *so* many times, she couldn't help it.

Razi blew the air out through his nose. He didn't like to be interrupted. "My hands to larger service and my health to better living for my . . ." Razi put up three fingers on one hand and one on the other. He studied his hands, waiting for the answer to come to him. "Three Cs and a W. Key?"

Brrrng, brrrng. A bicyclist swung around them and called out, "Passing on your right."

"My club, my community, my country and my world."

"Razi, that's perfect!" Keisha hugged him. "Say it just like that, okay?"

Razi bowed to the east and bowed to the west. "Okay, Key. I will."

They took each other's hands again and kept walking.

"Do you think Bob will wear his blue shirt tonight?" Grandma wondered out loud.

"Yes!" Razi shouted. He was still excited that he'd gotten the pledge right.

Grandma had a special interest in Big Bob, which Keisha *knew*, for a fact, because Grandma told her so as they sat on the porch looking at fireflies a few nights ago. Big Bob was Grandma's special some—

"Well, what do you think, Keisha?"

"I don't know," Keisha said. "I think he wore it last Saturday."

"He knows I like it," Grandma said. Grandma was talking and walking, but she had stopped seeing what was in front of her. Keisha had to tug her arm to keep her from running into a couple walking the other way.

"Aren't they sweet?" Grandma said. "I wonder how they met."

Then Grandma gave a big sigh and put her free hand against her cheek. They came to the last cross street before arriving at the center.

Grandma took hold of Keisha's shoulders. "Do you like these shoes with this dress?" she asked. "Now I'm not sure."

"Grandma!" Keisha said. "Look into my eyes. You. Are. Style."

"Thanks, sweetie." Grandma pinched her cheeks to make them rosy as apples. "Let's go get Razi inducted."

As they proceeded up the steps, Wen ran down to greet them. She was in one of the dresses her grandma Nei-Nei had sewed for her. It had a big bow in the back, and the ends of the bow fluttered around Wen as she ran toward them.

"You look like a kite," Razi told Wen.

"That's what I wanted to tell you, Razi. The box kite came! From my grandpa's family in China. Mr. Sanders delivered it today!"

"Ooh, can we go fly it, Grandma?" One of Razi's favorite things to do in the park was fly kites with Wen.

"Not now," Grandma said, smoothing her hands down the front of her dress. "Heavens to Betsey Johnson, Razi. Let's get your priorities straight. Bob is waiting in there."

Wen and the Carters were the first to arrive, but it didn't take long until everyone was there: Aaliyah, Jorge, Marcus, Zack, Zeke and a dozen other kids. Animals were very popular as a club choice this year. Mama scooped up baby Carmelo as soon as she saw Jorge and took him to the back where Daddy had baby Paulo. They were soon joined by Mr. Sanders, who had told Razi that morning at breakfast that he always liked to be present when his colleagues were in special ceremonies.

"What's a colleague?" Razi wanted to know.

"People who work together," Mr. Sanders said. "I deliver the mail and you take it in the house."

"Oh. Can we get ice cream after at Jersey Junction? Can we?"

Razi knew that Mr. Sanders *loved* Jersey Junction.

As soon as everyone was settled, they recited the Pledge of Allegiance.

Big Bob said, "The next order of business for our 4-H Wild 4-Ever Club is to recite the 4-H Pledge. But tonight we are inducting a new member into Wild 4-Ever, so first we'll do our activity—building nest platforms for next spring—then we'll have the business portion of the meeting, and we'll conclude by having Razi recite the pledge at his induction."

Razi stood up, his arms straight as arrows at his sides. "I pledge my head—"

"Not yet!" Keisha whispered, pulling him back down by his belt. Everyone giggled.

Fortunately, the next part of the meeting was the activity—building a nesting cone for mourning doves—and Razi helped Big Bob draw circles on the hardware mesh. The older kids got to cut out the circles with special wire-cutting scissors. After they did that, they cut out a pie-wedge-shaped piece so they could bend the mesh into a cone. Then they had to put electrical tape all around the sharp parts so the birds wouldn't get scratched.

Mourning doves were good at cooing, but they were not good at building nests. Their nests broke a lot. The children could take the cones home and put them in a good hiding place—a tree or a bush—six feet above the ground. That would help the mama's nest stay together.

As soon as the cones were stacked by the door and all the cleanup was done, Big Bob began the business portion of the meeting. Razi tried to stay still and quiet. He was sitting in one of the chairs, Keisha was next and Grandma was on the other side. This part of the meeting never lasted long. Keisha did spider fingers on Razi's back to help him stay still, then she let him play with his clip-on tie. After that, he made the church and the steeple with his fingers.

But enough was enough for Razi. During new business, he started waving his hand madly in the air. It looked like he was swatting at a bee or something. "Oh! Oh!" he said.

"Razi?" Big Bob pointed to him.

"I have a question," Razi said.

"Is it new business?" Big Bob asked.

"I think so," Razi said.

"Okay. Go."

"Why do pigs have such big noses and such little eyes?" Razi asked.

There was a big silence and a little look that passed between Grandma and Keisha. Keisha scooched one inch closer to Grandma and one inch farther away from Razi. Did he have to ask *every* question that came into his mind?

"I'm sorry, Razi. Help me understand how that connects to our subject tonight. Weren't we talking about birds?"

Another long silence. Razi looked around. He seemed, all of a sudden, miserable.

"Are you saying you want to put pig noses on our next agenda?" Bob asked.

"I think I know," Jorge said.

Everyone turned to look at Jorge.

Jorge *never* said anything. At least not that Keisha could remember. Jorge was the quietest, Wen was the second quietest and she was the third quietest in Wild 4-Ever.

"It's like birds have big beaks . . . like crows, and little eyes. Why is that?"

"Yes!" Razi said. "Why is that, Big Bob?"

"Well," Big Bob said. "I don't know. Alice. Do you have any suggestions?"

Grandma Alice saw that everyone was now looking at her. She sat up straight.

"Crows," she said, after thinking about it for a minute. She stopped. Then she started again. "Like other birds with big beaks, crows take advantage of the largeness . . . of their mouthparts to eat large things . . . dead things . . . such as those things found on the side of the road."

"That is disgusting," Aaliyah said. And she gave her "eeww" look.

"While it may be disgusting," Grandma replied, "it is opportunistic and therefore increases survival rates.

Nature, Miss Aaliyah, doesn't give a rattlesnake's rear end whether you think it's disgusting or not. It is what it is."

"Thank you, Alice." Grandma and Big Bob gazed into each other's eyes for a long time. "We are all smarter because of you."

Jorge raised his hand to ask when they were going to have the ceremony. "I have some things I want to ask Razi about animals," Jorge said. "But I'm not sure it's legal until he's a member."

Razi stood once again with his straight-arrow arms and everyone knew: this was his big moment. "I pledge my head to clearer thinking, my heart to greater loyalty, my hands to larger service and my health to better living. . . ."

Everyone held their breath.

Razi looked around wide-eyed. "For my club, my communitymyworldandmycountry," he finished.

"Hurrah!" Mr. Sanders shouted. And even though Razi put the W right in the middle of the three Cs, he got a standing ovation anyway.

Big Bob hurried things up to the end of the program, probably so he could spend more time with Grandma over refreshments, which, Keisha had to admit, had gotten a lot sweeter since their crush. Tonight it was cinnamon twists and apple tarts.

During refreshments, Razi got hugs and kisses and handshakes and claps on the back. He walked around on his tiptoes a lot.

Jorge told Razi, "You did a good job. I can never remember the 'hands to larger service' part. I don't know why. I guess I just don't want to give my hands to anybody. It seems weird."

"Me too," Razi said, pushing his shoulder into Jorge's shoulder as he bit down on his cinnamon twist.

Keisha let her shoulders relax. "Razi-Roo, I'm proud of you," she whispered.

"You're a poet and you didn't know it," Razi whispered back.

Chapter 6

"Carters' Urban Rescue!" Razi shouted into the phone on Monday morning. Technically, he wasn't supposed to answer the business line, but this morning he'd asked Mama, since he was now an official member of Wild 4-Ever, if he could and she'd said, "We'll see."

But Mama's hands were wet, Grandma was upstairs wiping off the lipstick she said was "too winter" and Keisha was wrestling Paulo into the stroller. Ever since he started pulling himself up and balancing, Paulo didn't like to be put in the stroller unless he was tired. So he arched his back and Keisha had her hands full to keep from dropping him onto the kitchen floor.

"Yes, we have a skunk, too!" Razi was saying. "He lives in the forest now. Under the big tree. Uh-huh uh-huh uh-huh . . . Mama!" Razi held out the phone. "It's for you!"

"I'm right here, Razi. Let him grip your fingers a little while, Ada. Grandma isn't down yet, so we have some time."

"Skunk tracks and cat tracks look alike, Mr. Peters. Can you see the toenails? . . . Well, they shouldn't be that hard to see if you got a good print. . . . Skunks cannot pull back their toenails, so they show right in the print. . . . All right, then. Can you see well enough to count the number of toes? . . . I understand. We will come by this morning. Mrs. Zadinkis invited me to come and pick some squash and beans for my pepper soup. . . . Thank you, I would love a tomato."

Mama had a pot of red pepper soup going on the stove most mornings, even when it was hot outside. Red pepper soup was made out of tomatoes and peppers and chicken broth. Then Mama added whatever vegetables she had around. Red pepper soup was for guests as well as for family. Anyone could drop by and have a little around dinnertime. Mrs. Zadinkis liked to drop by when she was in the neighborhood, so she gave Mama lots of good things from her garden. That's when Mama liked to say: it takes many raindrops to make the pond from which we drink.

Keisha was glad she hadn't finished putting Paulo in the stroller because now she had to buckle him into the car seat in back. He was just as stubborn about being put in his car seat. But Mama had a way with him. It was a short trip to the community garden and soon they were driving on the old track that had become a service road for people to load and unload their equipment and produce.

Mama loved to honk. It was a habit she learned

growing up in Nigeria, where people greeted each other with their horns. So as she honked her greeting, heads popped up all over the garden and hands waved to them. Keisha marveled at how much things could change in a garden from one week to the next. She and Wen and Aaliyah often rode by the community garden on their bikes, and it seemed like, once it got hot, the plants grew a foot every time. By this time in August, you couldn't even see the neighbors' yards that backed up to the garden because the sunflowers and hollyhocks were so tall. Straight rows of bush beans, long yellow peppers and juicy ripe tomatoes filled the gardens. Squash leaves, like big fans, grew right out onto the service road.

"Careful, Mama," Keisha said as they came close to squashing a basketball-sized watermelon that sat near the edge.

Mama pulled the truck over to the side and the children tumbled out.

Razi started to run in the direction of a big patch of daisies, but Mama caught his hand. "I need you with me."

He skipped alongside Mama as she went to the message board near the big toolshed. The shed was the gathering place for all the gardeners because it had the tools, potting soil, wood chips, watering cans and other things that they needed.

In the summertime, gardeners were in the garden all the time, but in the fall, when no one was around, children sometimes messed with the shed. Last fall, they'd broken the lock and left the tools all over the ground. Someone threw a rock and shattered the window. Though the window was due to be fixed, Mama was tsk-ing about the way the shed looked when her nose caught something in the air.

It seemed like everyone smelled it at the same time.

"That's stinky garbage," Razi said, plugging his nose.

"Mama?" Keisha caught up. "Skunk?"

Mama pursed her lips, thinking.

"How will we find Mr. Peters?" Keisha asked, trying to get her mind off the smell.

"The honking will spread the word. . . ." Mama sniffed again. "There is something about that smell. . . ." Mama touched her long fingers to her forehead, thinking.

Sure enough, an older lady in a plaid jumper and tennis shoes came over and put her hand on Mama's shoulder.

"I'm Mrs. Peters," she said. "You won't hurt it, will you? I've read terrible things on the Internet about what they do with nuisance animals."

Even though it was hot, Mrs. Peters hugged herself tight and shivered. "Though I have to agree, that

smell . . . is one of the most unpleasant. Even the tea
from my thermos smells like it now."

At the same time Mrs. Peters was talking, Razi
tugged on Mama's hand. She leaned over and whispered to him: "Where I can see you." Then she looked
at Keisha in a way that told her eldest daughter it was
her job to watch her brother.

Straightening up, Mama took Mrs. Peters's hand in both of hers and said, "Fayola Carter."

Mrs. Peters looked into Mama's eyes. "Jane."

"And Mr. Peters?"

"He's spraying the aphids off our mums." Mrs. Peters put her hand up over her eyes so she could see the far part of the garden. "Not with poison, mind you. Just a strong jet of water."

"Where did you spread the flour?" Mama asked.

"Over on this side of the shed."

As Mrs. Peters led the way, Mama asked Keisha, "Does this smell like skunk to you?"

Keisha thought about it. Skunks had a smell that was all their own. It was a little like rotten eggs, a little like dead things.

"Mama, look!" Razi was excited. "I found his hidey-hole."

No matter how many times Keisha told Razi it was called a den, Razi insisted that burrowing animals lived in hidey-holes. Call them what you wanted, Razi was an expert at finding them.

"As you can see"—Mrs. Peters pointed to the evidence—"this is where we spread the flour."

Mama kneeled down and examined the tracks. "You see, Mrs. Peters? No toenails and only four pad marks. You've had a cat travel through here."

"We have dozens of cats," Mrs. Peters said, laughing. "I'm not surprised about that."

Keisha noticed a few boards on the shed were peeled back and rotting, especially where Razi was on all fours. The entrance to the tunnel was not easy to see unless you were close to it. But when they bent down to look, Keisha could see that under the shed, the dirt was packed hard and the hole was wide.

No cat was responsible for this den.

She and Mama must have been thinking along the same lines because Mama said, "Wide for a skunk." Mama pulled Razi into her arms and away from the hole. "Maybe a woodchuck. Have you been missing any flowers?"

"Now that you mention it, Mr. Johnson lost a whole patch of petunias in one day. He thought the neighborhood children were picking them."

"Well, let's take a look. You should be able to tell the difference," Mama said. "If they are being eaten—" Razi broke free and squiggled farther into the hole. Keisha grabbed his hand. Grandma always said if you lost your trouble, Razi could find it.

"Come and jump rope with me, Razi," she said.

At the same time that she added, "You can count," Razi asked, "Can I count?"

No one liked it when Razi counted because he lost

track and then made up the numbers. Even when he used the mechanical counter that Aaliyah kept in her purse, he would get distracted by a butterfly or a passing car and stop pressing the counter. Still, Keisha remembered they'd left the ropes in the back of the truck and this would be a way to distract Razi while Mama talked to the Peterses and the other gardeners about woodchucks and skunks.

As they passed the truck on the way to the petunia patch, Keisha said to Mama, "It could be a skunk that lives down there. Maybe he moved in after someone else moved out."

"But why would he spray in his own den?" Mama wondered.

"That's what I was thinking . . . maybe someone or something found him in the shed and that's where the smell is coming from . . . not under the shed."

"There's something about that smell. . . ." Mama leaned in and got Keisha's jump rope. She also pulled out the live trap.

"Well, go and jump. I want to set this up and find Mr. Peters. And Mrs. Zadinkis. It looks like the patty-pan squash may be ripe."

"I don't want to jump; Key. I want to play hip-hopscotch," Razi said. "We could do it right here on the path." Keisha looked at the wide path. It would be easy to scratch out a hopscotch board with a stick, and she always carried her lucky marker in her pocket. It was a stone that fit just right in the palm of her hand. Mrs. Vanderest had let her paint it when the other kids were painting the big rocks.

"Okay, but *I* better draw it." Keisha dropped the rope and found a short, stubby stick. You had to make bigger squares for hip-hopscotch because the whole point was to dance inside the lines. You tossed your marker into a square, hopped to the square it landed on, called out a dance move and then danced it. Unlike counting for jump rope, Razi was very good at hip-hopscotch.

"Me first," Razi called as Keisha stood back to make sure she'd drawn it right.

"Okay, okay. Where's your marker?"

Razi held out both hands. "Please? I'll be careful. I promise."

Keisha put her blue rock with the purple dots in Razi's hand. "All right. If you promise."

Razi tossed the marker into the third square. He skipped on one foot to the square with Keisha's marker and called out, "MJ Step," then proceeded to dance the Michael Jackson step, where you put your hands in your pockets and slid out first one leg and then the other.

"Good job, Razi," Keisha said. As she watched her

brother skip to the next square, Keisha's mind skipped to the thought of a little skunk, curled up in its den. Skunks liked to burrow, and anything on the ground—logs, porches, sheds—was a good place for them to live. But it wasn't like a skunk to spray in its own den. What had happened to make it feel afraid?

"Drag turn with the disco arms!" Razi called out, and he waved his arms so hard he almost lost his balance.

Keisha felt a drop of sweat trickle down her temple. It was hot standing in the sun. She listened to Razi's skip-skip-skid on the ground.

"Heel-toe with a puppet walk."

That's it! Keisha thought. It's hot! Skunks are covered in fur. Why would it be curled up in its den? Skunks didn't always use dens in the summertime.

"Oh no! Key, I threw it too far."

Ooh. Keisha hated it when Razi interrupted her problem-solving process. "Well, go find it, Razi. You know it's my favorite. You promised."

Keisha looked down at her shoes again, trying to remember. It just didn't seem likely that a skunk would be curling up in a den when it was so hot out. This was the hottest time of the year. All of a sudden, Keisha saw Mama's shoes.

"The trap is set." Mama pulled Keisha to her and

wiped her daughter's face with the hem of her dress. "I put some grubs in a little bowl. Just what skunks like. But even if we don't catch a skunk, we should figure out what has been visiting. Those flowers were eaten, not picked, and woodchucks love to eat flowers." Mama picked up Keisha's rope and began rolling it up.

"Now, where is your brother? I don't want him anywhere near that trap because it's hard to set—"

Mama was interrupted by a very Razi-like scream. Keisha whirled around just in time to see Razi leap out of the bushes at the end of the garden and run toward them.

"He's going to bite me!" When he reached Mama, Razi grabbed the material of her dress and tried to hide himself in it.

"Razi. Little one, hush. Who is going to bite you?"

Razi was gulping for air. It didn't help that his head was buried in Mama's stomach.

"That bad dog. He was growling at me."

"I don't see a dog, Razi." Keisha looked in the direction Razi had come. The bushes were tall and tangled, and a honeysuckle vine filled with orange flowers grew across the top. There was no sign of a dog or any commotion beyond what Razi was causing.

"I was looking for Keisha's marker," Razi said, sniffing. "With the purple polka dots. I thought I saw it in there."

"Saw it in where, Razi?" Mama was examining Razi's arms. He was covered with little scratches, and there were seedpods in his hair.

"The bushes. That's where the bad doggy is. Bad dog! No!"

Razi had been afraid of dogs ever since he'd been knocked down by a big one at Millennium Park when he was three. It also didn't help that Harvey, the Bakers' dog, lunged at him every time they passed the Bakers' fence.

"Keisha, go see what this boy is talking about,"

Mama said, brushing the pods out of Razi's hair. "I'll take Razi with me to get our squash from Mrs. Zadinkis and meet you by the truck."

What Keisha wanted was her marker. She loved that marker. She walked slowly over to the spot where Razi came out of the bushes. This area got sun all day, so the vines of the trumpet honeysuckle were thick.

Just as she started to part the bushes to look in, Keisha did hear a low growl. It wasn't like Harvey's snapping scary growl. It was a small-sized growl.

As her eyes got used to the dark inside the bushes, Keisha saw a curly-haired dog, no bigger than a watermelon, lying on its side—panting. It tried to get up when it saw her. It growled again. Keisha had been around animals enough to know this was not an I'm-going-to-bite-you growl but a defensive growl.

"What is it, Keisha?" Keisha felt Mama's warm hand on her back.

"It's hurt, Mama. Its front legs are funny. And it has some big scratches on its behind. They might be bites."

Mama parted the bushes further and took a close look. "This dog needs medical attention right away," she said. "I'm going to get the cell phone out of the truck and call Bob. I'll get a box and a towel, too."

Chapter 7

The next morning, Grandma clomped up the basement stairs, her arms full of supplies. "They don't call it *Mephitis mephitis* for nothing," she said, to no one in particular. "I bought two quarts of tomato juice at the Dollar Store yesterday. The rest of the ingredients should be here in my secret stash. . . ." She rummaged through the box she'd brought up. "Where's that hydrogen peroxide?"

"There's one bottle in the medicine cabinet and you're borrowing some more from Mrs. Sanders. You just called to ask," Keisha said. Keisha and Razi were sitting at the kitchen table, coloring. Keisha had her favorite drawing book next to her—*How to Draw Baby Animals*. It was opened to the puppy page.

"'Puppies have larger heads compared to their bodies than full-sized dogs,'" Keisha read aloud as she sketched.

Razi was working on a picture from a coloring book they'd given him at his Safety Town class. He was coloring all the police officers purple. He started a song: "*Me-phi-tis me-phi-tis*. It smells like your armpits!"

"Has Mama called yet?" Keisha asked Grandma. Mama and the baby were at the community garden checking on the skunk trap. Mama had also promised that she would swing by the vet clinic at the Humane Society and check on the little dog they'd brought in yesterday afternoon. Keisha wondered if anyone had claimed her yet.

"No, not in the thirty seconds since you asked me the last time. Where is the Z-Team? I can't do this without hydrogen peroxide."

"*Me-phi-tis me-phi-tis me-phi-tis.*" All Razi cared about was his new-sounding word.

"What does that mean, Grandma?" Keisha had to almost shout to be heard over Razi's noise. She knew it was a Latin name, one that helped people all over the world no matter what language they spoke identify an animal, but the words usually meant something.

"In Latin it means 'stink,' " Daddy said, coming up from the basement with the box that their new computer had arrived in. "Mom, how many times have I told you not to climb the stepladder in the basement? You could fall."

"That's what my gentle yoga class is for," Grandma said. "Look." Grandma put her hands over her head and bent way backward. "I call this cat-diving-backward-into-pool," she said. "I've got the body of a twenty-year-old. Razi, give me a hand here."

Razi was good at pushing Grandma back to her starting point. He stood on his tippy-toes and pushed on her shoulders until she was in her spaceship-heading-to-the-moon pose.

Using his pocketknife, Daddy began to cut the flaps off the box. "I guess they named it *Stinky stinky* because when they spray, skunks smell so bad that's all you can think about."

He walked over to Grandma's ingredient box and looked at the contents. "Hmmm . . . vinegar, baking soda. Where's the hydrogen peroxide?"

"That's the million-dollar question," Grandma said. "I thought the Z-Team was coming over with it."

"If you call Mama on her cell," Keisha said as she continued to color soft brown puppy ears, "she can pick some up at Perkins Drugstore by the vet clinic. Daddy, did you know she's going to check up on the dog?"

Before Mr. Carter had a chance to answer, Grandma said: "Who's going to check up on Mrs. Sampson? That's what I want to know."

Keisha made extra curls on her puppy's ears. From what Mrs. Sampson had told them, the baby crow was doing just fine, but Keisha agreed that Mrs. Sampson could use some checking up on, too.

"Her milk was sour," she said. "I could smell it all the way in the dining room."

"You should have opened the refrigerator. Ooooweee!" Grandma plugged her nose.

"We can check on Mrs. Sampson when we check on the baby crow," Daddy said. "If she's as good a nurse as she says she is, that fledgling might be able to be released this afternoon."

"Then what will happen, Daddy?"

"Then he'll fly away and join the others. Or at least he'll start."

"Listen, Mom. As long as we're waiting for Fayola to see if she got a skunk, I'm going to walk over to the hardware store. I never got a chance to stop the other day, and I need some chicken wire. . . . Those ducklings are getting ready to fly the coop and they belong in the park, not on Horton Street."

"We're the welcoming committee! For the skunk." Zeke knocked on the door as he was opening it. He put the bottle of hydrogen peroxide on the counter.

"About time, boys," Daddy said. "All we have to do is get the pen ready. Keisha has a good feeling we caught one in the trap last night. Then we have to go check on that fledgling. Come on, Razi, Keisha. . . ." Daddy led the way back outside, holding the box in front of him. "Let's get this pen set up before I take off."

"I'm coming!" Razi dropped his crayons on the floor and ran after Daddy. Keisha scooped them up and followed Daddy and the boys into the garage.

"I hate to use one of our crates because you can't get the smell out if the skunk sprays. So, Razi, you get started with the pumpkin cutter and saw a door hole in this box. I'll run over to the hardware store and be right back."

Keisha kissed Daddy as Razi sat down on the floor and started sawing away.

Zeke bent over Razi. "I think that hole is too small for a skunk."

"Give it to me," Zack said. "I can make it bigger." Zack loved to show off how strong he was. He took the box and started tearing away the piece Razi had begun to cut.

"No, Zack! That was the front door!" Tears spilled down Razi's cheeks. "His friends had to knock and then he would say 'come in' and then they would bring presents and then he would have a party! But now it's all wrong."

Grandma opened the back door and hollered out: "Attention, Animal Rescue Team! We have a skunk! Fayola just called. They're on their way."

Keisha kneeled down by Razi. She hugged him so he could wipe his tears on her T-shirt. She could see what

Razi was trying to do. He was trying to make a door, like a cat door, with two cuts so that the skunk would have to push his way in. But now Zack had torn a big hole for the opening. Razi took the piece of cardboard Zack had ripped out and put it under his bottom as if to make believe it had never happened.

"I have an idea," Keisha said, tugging the piece of cardboard back out. "Let's make that the back of the house. We can tape this back on. I don't think the skunk will care. Then we'll cut two bigger slits and bend the top of the front door backward and forward so it's easy to push."

"It could be a window," Razi said, rubbing his eyes. "But just a little one. So he can peek out."

"Okay, I'll tear off a little piece and then we'll tape it back on." Zack was happy to have something to do to make Razi feel better. Keisha called inside to Grandma for the duct tape.

"What else do we need?" Grandma asked after she came outside and handed the roll to Keisha. She still had her apron on. Aprons were OL, but necessary when you were cooking up a pot of skunk smell remover.

"Let's go see." Grandma led the way out of the garage into the part of the backyard where the pens were kept.

"Dirt!" Razi said. "Skunks like to dig."

All eyes traveled from the skunk enclosure to the side of the house. "Do they dig or do they fling?" Grandma asked.

"They fling!" Razi threw his hands up in the air. Skunks were a Razi kind of animal. "I'll get him some sand from my sandbox."

An "and then" story popped into Keisha's head. It wasn't just little brothers who could tell them. "If this skunk decides to burrow under his den box and then sand gets on the side of the house and the clean laundry on the line and then Mama sees what the skunk has done and then she says something like, 'One must row in the boat in which one finds oneself,' we're going to end up doing a lot of cleaning up."

Grandma had the last word. "No need to explain your mama's clean habits, dear. We'll keep the sand in the sandbox and see if this skunk can make a dent in our clay soil. What else do we need to make the skunk happy? He'll only be here a few days, until we make sure he's healthy and find a good place to release him."

"Do skunks like toys?" Zeke asked.

"Maybe my dump truck!" Razi said. "If he can't dig, he can excavate."

Razi had recently discovered the joys of earth-moving.

Grandma looked thoughtful. "Sounds good, though I don't know if his paws can handle the levers."

"He'll need a bowl of water," Keisha reminded her.

"Well, let's set it up, because as soon as Fred gets back, we have to go see our feathered friend. I've got a feeling today is his big day."

"You mean the crow? Can we go, too?" Zeke asked.

Ever since the word "murder" had come up, the Z-Team wanted to be in on the crow action.

Razi tugged on Grandma's apron. "I'm hungry, Grandma. When is lunch?"

"You already had lunch, Razi, and we promised Wen

and Aaliyah they could come," Grandma told the Z-Team. "There's not enough room in the truck."

"We could ride in the truck bed," Zeke offered.

"Like Mr. Cannon's hunting dogs," Zack said.

"They fall down a lot," Zeke said, remembering. "Maybe we could just double-buckle."

"Dunch, then. When's dunch?" Razi was still tugging. He didn't care much about eating, but he didn't like grumblies in his tummy, either.

Grandma reached into her apron pocket and pulled out a handful of Nilla wafers. "Dunch," she said, handing them to Razi, and turning to Zack and Zeke: "You know the rules."

"Then we'll take our bikes and meet you!"

Their conversation was interrupted by Mama honking her greetings.

"Well, you're not going to do anything right now because non-essential personnel must go to the house immediately."

Chapter 8

The Z-Team were the first ones up the back steps. Razi was *not* essential personnel, but he ran over to the truck anyway. Keisha opened the truck door and started to unbuckle Paulo.

"I would have been back sooner," Mama said, climbing out of the truck, "but the baby had to travel from one set of arms to the other, all the way to the end of the garden."

"Did the skunk spray anyone before you got there?" Keisha asked. Paulo was asleep, his little head pillowed by the car seat strap.

"No, but he's not too happy. A lot of chit-chit-chitting. Why don't you take these zucchini and patty-pan squash into the house while I get him settled? Tell the Z-Team they can watch from the window, but they don't need to press their noses against my clean glass. I'll put the skunk's cage in the pen with the door open. If he comes out, they can see him from the window."

"But I want to give him a traditional Nigerian greeting and inquire after his family," Razi said as he disappeared into the bed of the truck. Keisha saw the black fabric of the superhero cape flutter as Razi tried to get a peek. Mama often brought Razi's cape along and draped it over the crate to give the animals a sense of calm.

"Razi Carter. Get out of there. What are you doing?" Mama scolded.

At the sound of Mama's stern voice, Paulo started crying. His eyes were still closed. Keisha moved his head to undo the strap. "Did you see the puppy, Mama? Is she going to be okay?" Gently, Keisha eased the baby out of the seat into her arms.

"Not now, Ada. I'll tell you later. Razi, come out. If you upset him, you'll get sprayed. Skunks don't know anything about the way people say hello."

"No!" Razi said. "Not for you."

"I said get down here, Razi. Now!"

"I just wanted to ask after his family, like you and Daddy do when you meet a new friend." Razi looked like he was ready to cry again. It was a tearful day.

"You can," Mama said. "When he's had a chance to settle in. Now go up into the kitchen with Zack and Zeke and tell them to be still as statues and wait."

Razi climbed out of the truck. Keisha knew right away he'd done something he shouldn't have because he was pinching his lips together. She fit the baby on her hip, held out her hand to Razi and they went inside.

"I found a better way to make friends," Razi told her,

licking his fingers. Keisha thought about asking, but decided maybe she didn't want to know.

"The skunk has a scratch on his nose," Razi informed Keisha.

"Was it bleeding?"

"No, it was an old one." Razi pulled open the back door and stuck his knee in the air. "Like this one. It's a healed scratchy."

"You mean a scar," Keisha corrected. Razi was pointing to a scar he'd earned last summer after jumping from the swing set.

As they came through the door, Grandma lifted her head from the steaming pot of skunk stink remover. Her cheeks were flushed and the hair at her temples was all curly.

"Razi, look in that bag over there and pull out the Talbots sweater I scored from New 2 You. It's one hundred percent cashmere in my favorite color."

"Mmmm." Razi lifted a bright pink sweater out of the bag. "It's soft."

Grandma glanced over at Razi, who was rubbing the sweater on his face like a washcloth. "Go on," she said. "As long as it's all steamy in here, I might as well wash it and put it on the line."

Razi put the sweater on his head and breathed in. "It smells like flowers."

"Well, don't make an occupation out of it. Bring it here so I can read the washing instructions. Keisha, where are my glasses?"

"Up in your room." Keisha took the sweater from Razi.

"I'll read the instructions, Grandma. It says 'dry-clean only.' "

"I will not."

Keisha thought to remind Grandma that you couldn't talk back to a label.

"Read it again. I think it says 'hand-wash in cold water and line-dry.' "

"Mama's moving the skunk!" Razi was hopping up and down.

"I can't see a thing!" Zeke protested. Grandma's steam had fogged up the window and Zeke was using his tummy to wipe a clear circle on the pane of glass.

"Quick, everybody, let's practice in case we get sprayed." Zack shouted to be heard over Zeke's shouting. The boys all grabbed pot lids and started to fight over which was the biggest.

Grandma covered her ears. "You could have warned me," she called out. "I've got the amplifiers in."

"If he sticks his butt in your face, do this." Zeke demonstrated by turning his face to the side and holding the pot lid in front of it.

While the boys wrestled with the pot lids, Keisha held Paulo tight to her shoulder—Grandma always said he could sleep through the Battle of Burgundy—and watched her mother pull the metal cage covered in black fabric to the edge of the truck and lift it. Wild animals had no experience with being moved around in cages. Keisha could see Mama crooning to the skunk as she set the cage down in the enclosure. Slowly, Mama lifted the metal bar and let the cage door swing open so the skunk was free to leave the cage and go into the pen.

"I'm getting the trash can lid." Razi ran to the garage door.

"I'll get the snow dish!" Zack ran after him.

This had to stop! Keisha whistled through her teeth—high and shrill—just like Daddy taught her and Grandpa Wally Pops taught him. Worked every time. The boys froze. Paulo opened his eyes and looked at Keisha, startled, then he closed his eyes again.

"Listen, you crazy boys. You start clanging those pot lids together and you'll definitely get sprayed. The two things that really upset skunks are loud noises and—"

"Rap music," Razi called out. "Especially the kind with the bad words."

"No, Razi, that's Mama. Great horned owls."

"Okay, okay." Zeke put his pot lid on the table. "Can we go out if we promise no banging?"

"No!"

But Razi wasn't listening. He was too excited. He skipped outside with his hands covering his mouth. Keisha couldn't accomplish much with Paulo in her arms, so she took a moment to dash upstairs and lay him in his crib. When she came back down, she used her fist to swipe a peephole in the window. Razi had gotten down on his hands and knees so he could see into the darkened cage. Mama scooped him up and brought him back inside.

"Now the little one gets settled," she said. "He's frightened and he can smell us nearby. Speaking of little ones—" Mama looked around.

"He's in his crib," Keisha said.

"Well, normal life has to resume at some point," Grandma said, pushing past them, out the back door and down the stairs, and marching toward the laundry pole with the damp sweater she'd been washing out in the sink. Grandma didn't even glance in the direction of the skunk as she clipped her sweater to the line.

Bustling back inside, she said: "If we froze all operations just because we got a new animal, where would that leave us? Hungry and without fashionable clothes is my bet. Now, if you please, someone's got to think of dinner around here."

"We're going to have soup, Alice." Mama held up

another bag of vegetables she'd brought from the garden.

"Yes, but what about the sides?"

"Soup doesn't have sides," Zeke said. "It's too slippery."

"I'm talking about sides like Texas toast or cottage cheese with pineapple."

Ick. Cottage cheese. Keisha was listening, but she stayed near the window and kept her eyes trained on the covered metal cage. Twice, she'd seen a little pointed snout peek out and sniff the air. She was sending mental messages to the skunk that it was okay to move from the cage with its uncomfortable metal bars along the bottom to the dirt floor of the pen to the nice dark cozy box.

"You could have s'mores," Zeke suggested. "They're a good side dish."

"Let's have dessert for dinner," Razi agreed. "And lemonade for dessert!"

"I don't think so, hummingbird." Keisha wiped some Nilla wafer crumbs from Razi's chin. "You've had enough sweets."

"Wen and Aaliyah are here." Zeke pressed his finger to the window, making a fresh print.

The children watched as Wen and Aaliyah stashed their bikes against the side of the garage and kneeled down to pull something out of Wen's backpack. Aaliyah wanted to tug it out, but Wen pushed her away. Wen almost never pushed.

"What's that?" Razi's attention and everyone else's were now on what was in Wen's backpack, but Keisha had not forgotten about the little skunk. She could see half his body now, turning in one direction and then another, trying to figure out what to do.

"What are they doing?" Zeke asked.

"It's the kite!" Razi shivered with happiness. "Wen's grandpa's family sent her a kite from China. He made a box with no bottom. She's gonna show me how to fly it." Sure enough, when the girls stood up, Wen had a roll of string and Aaliyah was holding what looked like a poster glued to sticks. She pointed to a spot over by

the garage and Aaliyah took off running. The string un-wound off the spool. Aaliyah loved an excuse to run. She was the Langston Hughes Elementary School record holder in the 100-yard dash.

"Doesn't look like much to me," Zack said. "It's not even pointy."

"It's a box with no bottom, like Razi said. That's how it catches the air. Wen told me about it, too." Zeke pushed his brother with his shoulder to get a better look.

"But that's not a box. That's flat," Zack replied.

Keisha worried that if Aaliyah ran too close to the pen, she might get the same result as a bunch of pan-banging boys. The little skunk must have run into the box or back into the cage because he was nowhere to be seen.

Aaliyah put her arm between the two layers of the kite and popped it open. All of a sudden it looked like a long tall box with no bottom. Red and green streamers fluttered in the breeze.

"See, I told you it was a box," Zeke said.

Just as Aaliyah held up the kite to look inside, Wen must have reached the end of the string because the kite jumped out of Aaliyah's hand and shot up to the sky. The kite was in the air, but where had Aaliyah gone? She must have run all the way around to the front yard.

"Wait for me, Aaliyah," Razi shouted. Before Mama could catch the tail of his shirt, he ran out the back door and disappeared around the side of the house.

"That poor little skunk," Mama said. "In all this commotion I wonder where he went."

"I think he's behind the box," Keisha said. "No! There he is!" The skunk must have been scared stiff because he was standing frozen in the middle of the pen.

"Uh-oh." Grandma Alice had left off preparing the side dish and come over to the window. She leaned in, resting her chin on Keisha's shoulder. "He's stomping his feet."

"What's that mean?" Zeke asked.

"It's what skunks do when they are trying to warn an attacker," Keisha said. But who was the attacker? It couldn't be Aaliyah or Razi. They were on the other side of the house. Wen was far enough away from the pen and she wasn't moving, either, just watching the kite as it traveled across the sky.

"Now he looks like he's growling," Zack said. "His butt's going up! His butt's going up! He's getting ready to let go. Man the pot lids!"

"Settle down." Keisha grabbed Zack's arm. "We're inside. Skunk spray doesn't go through glass." Her eyes scanned the backyard. What was the skunk scared of?

"Look! Aaliyah's coming back."

"He's probably scared of Aaliyah," Zeke said. "She's scary when she runs right at you in gym."

"But it wasn't her a minute ago. She was in the front yard."

A shadow passed over the lawn.

Suddenly Keisha knew. "Oh no, look up. It's the kite."

"Why would the skunk be afraid of a kite?" Zeke asked.

"He's not. He's afraid of the shadow. I read about it when I was waiting for Mr. Peters to come back to the phone. Owls fly overhead, casting big shadows just like that kite. A skunk's instinct tells him to get ready to defend himself when he sees a big shadow like that."

"But Aaliyah's going to get the 'stinct' part of it if she's not careful," Grandma said.

The skunk had bared his teeth and was raising his rear end even higher in the air. Aaliyah ran closer. Keisha knew her friend would want to run by the window so everyone could admire the way she was flying the kite.

"He's gonna do it! He's gonna spray Aaliyah," Zeke shouted.

"No way. Aaliyah's too fast for the stink," Zack said.

"Yeah. She's faster than a speeding stink bomb."

"Boys," Mama said. "Settle down."

Aaliyah ran back across the driveway and saw the skunk, hissing and looking toward her. She was so surprised, she stopped dead in her tracks, turned around and looked up at the kids.

Now *all* noses were pressed against Mama's clean window. When Aaliyah stopped, so did the kite. It fell toward the earth and got tangled in the branches of the horse chestnut tree. Wen, who'd been standing by her bike the whole time watching the kite's progress, pressed her hands to her face. Keisha could see how upset she was. Her kite traveled all the way from China only to get stuck in a tree on its first flight?

Razi ran to the tree and jumped up, trying to grab the lowest branch. He knew he wasn't allowed to climb that tree!

Keisha cracked open the back door. She didn't

know which was worse: Aaliyah covered in skunk spray or Razi dangling from the horse chestnut tree. But Razi couldn't jump high enough to reach a branch, so he gave up and ran over to Aaliyah. When he saw the skunk, he put his arms around her to protect her.

"He's gonna blow his stinky stuff on you," Keisha heard Razi warn Aaliyah.

"Oh no, he's not." Aaliyah put her hands on her hips and stared down the skunk. "If I get skunk spray on me, Moms will never allow me out, and it is *my* summer vacation."

Keisha knew skunks didn't understand English, but she was pretty sure he felt the anger coming from Aaliyah. He chattered his teeth and raised and lowered his tail as if to say he would nip her if she came any closer.

"Don't you raise your behind to me, mister! What do I look like to you? You're not even as big as my cat."

"Oh no." Keisha put her head back inside the door and said to Mama, "She's telling off the skunk."

"Go get that child while there's still time. Skunks don't spray unless they have to. You may be able to avoid a disaster."

"That girl doesn't have the sense she was born with," Grandma said. "I told her all about skunk spray."

Keisha thought about explaining to Mama and Grandma that it didn't matter what the threat was; if someone insulted Aaliyah, she had to stand and defend herself. Keisha was about to run out and get Aaliyah when, suddenly, the skunk's tail went stiff and his little body jerked like he was shooting jets of spray.

Keisha plugged her nose and slammed the door shut. Grandma turned the key in the lock. Aaliyah made an ugly face and ran toward the back door with Razi right behind her. Keisha looked around for Wen, but she couldn't see her. Maybe she was running, too.

"They're not allowed in this house until they've

been decontaminated," Grandma Alice said. "It will cover every surface. We'll never get the smell out."

Aaliyah was pounding on the back door. "Yuck! Let us in."

"Stall her," Grandma said. "I'll get the rubber gloves and Grandma's special patented skunk stink remover." Grandma grabbed the pot off the stove and splashed some of the stink remover around the kitchen as she went to find a bucket.

"Oh," Mama said, rubbing her temples. "Sometimes the cure is worse than the illness."

"That stuff stinks, too." Zeke joined Keisha by the door.

"Let." *Bang.* "Us." *Bang.* "In." *Bang!* Aaliyah pounded on the door.

"I can't," Keisha said. "Not until you've been decontaminated."

"What are you talking about? He didn't spray me! Don't you think I'd know if I'd been sprayed by a skunk?"

Keisha opened the door a crack and Zeke helped it along. "C'mon, Zack. Wanna smell some skunk stink?"

"I can't find my washing pail," Grandma said. "I'll just have to take it in the pot." The soup pot was getting heavy for Grandma. She had her rubber apron and gloves on now and was struggling toward the door. Zeke held it open for her and she came down the steps slowly, sloshing a bit of her cure on her apron with every step. Mama rushed by them to the skunk's pen.

"You can put your pot down, Alice. This isn't skunk spray." Mama sniffed the air. "But there is something. Razi Carter? Come to me, please."

"Yes, Mama." Razi had his hands under his shirt, a sure sign he'd been doing something with them he wasn't supposed to.

Keisha looked for the skunk. It must have retreated back into the cloth-covered cage. That was probably the only place it felt safe.

"Razi, what do I see sprinkled around this pen? Are these crumbs? Did you give something to this skunk?" Mama asked.

"I gave him a traditional Razi greeting."

"And what is that?"

"That's not skunk spray I smell," Grandma Alice announced as if she were the only one who could make the decision. "That's the result of an intact *flatus apparatus*."

Everyone looked at Grandma.

"Huh?" Zeke, Zack and Aaliyah said at the same time.

Grandma straightened and said in her Professor Alice voice: "An odor resulting from an intact *flatus apparatus* and caused by an upset stomach or other digestive problem."

"Razi?" Mama was looking at Razi with her *tell-me-the-truth-no-ifs-ands-or-buts* look.

"I didn't give them to him . . . he took them!" Razi pulled his hands out from underneath his shirt and balled up his fists like he was ready for a fight.

Mama tilted her head to the side. "Now, now, we are not blaming you. We just want to know—"

"My Nilla wafers. The ones Grandma Alice gave me. I was going to break off a little piece, but I dropped one, and he reached through the bars and got it."

Razi puffed his cheeks and let out a big blow of air, relieved he didn't have to keep that secret anymore. "Then I dropped the other ones in his cage and he ate those, too."

"Dropped them in by accident? Or on purpose?"

"He likes Nilla wafers!"

"Didn't you say you lured him into the cage at the garden with grubs, Fayola?" Grandma asked.

Mama nodded.

"Aha . . . ohhh . . . ooooweee! That's grub and Nilla wafer flatus. No wonder it smells so bad. But no permanent harm done. The fresh air will take care of it all and the Z-Team can help me bottle up Grandma's special patented skunk stink remover for another day."

"Awww, do we have to?" Zack whined.

"I want to fly Wen's kite," Zeke said.

"Where is Wen?" Keisha wondered.

"Up here!" Wen called. She had climbed halfway up the horse chestnut tree to free her beautiful kite.

"I want to climb the tree with Wen!" Razi shouted.

Mama was rubbing her temples again.

"Boys," Grandma Alice said, putting a hand on each of the twins' backs and directing them to the steps. "There will come a day when you realize the important wisdom that your elders carry with them. Until then, get inside and grab the funnels. We'll bottle this stuff up, and when we're finished, we'll make some indoor s'mores."

Chapter 9

By the time Grandma's skunk stink remover was bottled, the Z-Team had been called home to help Mrs. Sanders pot up seedlings, and Wen and Aaliyah had to go to the library for TAT (Tuesday-afternoon tutors), where they read with the little kids and helped them pronounce the big words. Grandma promised the Z-Team they could roast marshmallows over the fire pit that night, which was much better than indoor s'mores anyway.

To help Razi's grumblies, Mama whipped up a batch of her ginger cake and threw in some bananas to roast while it baked. Daddy came home with the chicken wire and Razi ran outside to be with him. Keisha could hear them through the window as they worked to make the sides of the duckling enclosure higher.

"Can I help, Daddy?" Razi asked. "Please?"

Thwack went the staple gun.

"Quack-quack," the ducklings replied.

"Quack-quack-quack." Razi imitated the ducks. "I did it just like Jorge!"

Mama, Keisha, Grandma and a still-sleepy Paulo sat

in the kitchen waiting for Mama's ginger cake and roasted bananas to be done. Grandma was leaning back in her chair, a slice of cucumber on each eye. Grandma had been out late the night before with Big Bob. The cucumber slices were to make her eyes less puffy. Everyone knew puffy eyes were OL.

It felt warm and dozy. A stranger walking down the street would never know that the Carters and their friends had just had a close call with a skunk and freed a kite from a tree, unless they heard Razi reliving it for Daddy.

"...and then Mama said the cure was worse

than the illness and then Grandma said it was the flaparatus—"

"The what? Wait a minute. That's my cell phone."

Keisha perked up. Daddy hardly ever gave out his cell phone number.

As she tried to listen, Keisha noticed Grandma Alice nodding off. Keisha moved Grandma's juice to the center of the table. Sometimes, when Grandma dozed off, she woke up with a start, caught the parasol sitting in her pomegranate juice and knocked the whole thing over.

Mama handed Paulo to Keisha and checked the oven. A whoosh of even warmer air swirled into the room. "I think it's just about done."

"Is Grandma sleeping?" Keisha whispered to Mama as she shifted the sweaty baby to her other knee.

"Your grandma was up late last night," Mama said, removing the cake from the oven. "She had a date."

"Huh?" Grandma sat up and the cucumbers fell on the table.

Even though Mama whispered, too, Grandma must have had the amplifiers in.

"It was all business," Grandma said.

Mama tsk-tsked. "It was still late. Keisha, put the baby in his high chair."

"I'm afraid I have bad news," Daddy said as he

walked into the kitchen. Razi was behind him, his fingers in Daddy's belt loops.

"I gave Mrs. Sampson my cell phone number," he said. "That was her. I think the gray just got grayer."

Baby Paulo squeaked and slapped his hands flat on his high chair tray, much like a baby bird. He must have smelled the roasted banana. If you waited for a roasted banana to cool, you could scoop it right from the skin.

"Don't tell me she released the bird before you checked him." Mama tapped the top of the cake to make sure it was done in the center.

"She didn't let it go. In fact, she doesn't plan to let it go."

"Excuse me?"

"She wants to keep it for a pet."

"Be serious," Grandma said. "A crow?" She put two new cucumber slices on her eyes and tried to relax back in her chair again.

"A crow doesn't make a cuddly pet," Keisha said. "What she really needs is a puppy. A soft curly furry one that sits on her lap and licks her hand."

"Or a kitty," Razi said. "Kitties have little hairs on their tongue so they can clean their fur."

"This is what happens when you explore the gray area, Fred." Mama handed Daddy a slice of steaming ginger cake.

Daddy rubbed his bristly chin. "You're right, Fayola. I didn't think about the lonely part. Lonely is a powerful feeling."

"Well, I'll tell you who's going to be lonely, and that's the crow. Those two need to stick to their own kind." Grandma took a cucumber slice off her eye and bit into it. "Is that clock right? Two p.m. already? I've got to get going. Bob's picking me up in the Bonneville and we're going out to Crane's Pie Pantry. I am so hungry for rhubarb-apple pie, I've been dreaming about it lately."

"Knock, knock. Just taking my afternoon break and I thought I smelled . . ." Mr. Sanders peeked around the door before letting himself in. "Ah yes! Ginger cake."

"Please come in, Mr. Sanders," Mama said. She sliced a big piece of cake and set it on a plate.

"Doug, can I ask you something? Have you been able to deliver mail to Mrs. Sampson's mailbox yet?" Daddy handed Mr. Sanders a fork and a napkin.

"Goodness, heavens no." Mr. Sanders took a big bite of cake. He mmm'ed and swallowed. "I can't get near the thing. I give it to her neighbor, Mrs. Hogue, which isn't strictly legal, but it solves the problem for a short time."

"I bet you call that the gray area," Grandma said. "It's not legal, but it makes sense for a short time. Hmmmph." She took another bite of cucumber.

"Well, we are trying to do our job, Mrs. Carter, and there are certain instances—"

"My son here has gotten lost in the gray area because Mrs. Sampson wants to keep her crow as a pet."

"And so the adult crows will never know it's back out in the big wide world?" Mr. Sanders had been ready to take another big bite of cake, but he set it back on his plate. "Oh dear. That would be a problem."

"Let go and sit down, bucko," Daddy said to Razi. "I want to eat my cake, too." Razi unhitched himself from Daddy's belt loops and pulled up a chair.

Daddy took a bite. "Mmm. Razi, you need to try this batch. Oh, it's so good. What time do you get finished today, Doug? Would you be willing to go with us to try to convince Mrs. Sampson that keeping the crow is not a good idea?"

Another piece of cake traveled up to Mr. Sanders's mouth and back down to his plate. Keisha noticed that his duties to the United States Postal Service came even before his love for Mama's cooking.

"I will. This really has to end," he said. "There's nothing in our rule book about crows, but if birds fall under the ruling of nuisance animals, they have to be eliminated."

"What a shame," Mama said. "Those crows are only trying to protect the baby they think is still inside. Will you take a piece for the boys, Mr. Sanders?"

"If you could wrap it up, I know they would be most grateful for the home cooking, Mrs. Carter."

"Of course." Mama wrapped a slice of cake in an old dishcloth that Keisha knew he would return clean in the next day or two.

Mr. Sanders said good-bye and hurried off to finish delivering his mail.

"Alice, please have a piece," Mama said, cutting another one. "You look bony to me."

"I'm not bony. I'm svelte, Fayola. And I'm waiting for the pie. I told you. I've been dreaming about it."

"Been dreaming about pie, Mom? Or is it Bob you've been dreaming about?" Daddy asked.

"Very funny, mister. That's enough of that."

"Oh my goodness." Keisha sat up straight. "In all the skunk excitement, I almost forgot. You were going to give me an update on the puppy!"

"Keisha Carter, you've got puppies on the brain." Grandma tossed the rest of the cucumbers in the compost bucket and downed her pomegranate juice. "Didn't you see her gray beard? That dog is no puppy. I'd say she's seven at least. That's about fifty in dog years."

Mama handed Keisha a spoon and a dish of roasted banana for the baby. Keisha scooped up a spoonful and let it steam, waiting until it cooled enough to put in Paulo's mouth. She decided to ignore Grandma's comment.

"Grandma knows more than I do," Mama said. "Grandma?"

"Well, if you must know, that's what Bob and I were doing last night. Dr. Wendy had to put a cast on her leg. She's concerned about the tendon damage. And the mats in her fur! We watched a Marx Brothers and a Charlie Chaplin movie just combing out the burs. Mats and bad breath are very OD."

"OD?" Mama asked.

"Old dog," Grandma said. "We got her a new collar to snazzy her up a bit."

"Did the doggy bite you?" If the dog bit Grandma, then Keisha knew it was a deal breaker for her little brother.

"No, she's got the sweetest temper after what she's been through, poor thing. They might have to amputate her leg, and who's going to want a seven-year-old three-legged dog with bad teeth?"

Keisha had to sit on her hands while Grandma described how good the pale blue collar looked against the dog's curly, cocoa-colored fur.

"Bob even drew a little message on her cast that said, 'To know me is to love me.' It's all in the presentation." Grandma glanced at the clock again. "Speaking of presentation, I've got to get some lipstick on!"

Keisha broke off a tiny piece of ginger cake and let it dissolve on her tongue. It was cool enough, so she broke off a piece for Paulo and put it on his tray.

Grandma rummaged through her purse for her lipstick and her compact.

"That's a new color," Keisha said, watching Grandma put the lipstick on.

"Gypsy Love," Grandma said. "Maureen at the beauty counter at Perkins Drugstore said it was perfect for my skin tone. Bob's taking me out for ice cream after we have pie. Hudsonville has much better ice cream than Crane's."

"Hmmmph." Razi started to pout. "You can't do pie before and ice cream after! That's two desserts in one day. That's not allowed. Mama, I want to do pie before and ice cream after. Can I, Mama? Just once? Pretty please?"

"You might get something in a take-home box," Grandma said, stretching her lips wide and using her fingernail to scrape off everything that was outside the lines. "It depends if I can remember how many times you kicked me in church last Sunday."

Razi was still sitting in the kitchen chair, but he made his legs and arms rigid. He stayed frozen that way for a few seconds. Paulo banged his tray, making the ginger cake bounce. Keisha poked the spoonful of roasted banana into his mouth.

"Bzzzzrrrrr. Bzzzzrrrr," Paulo said, letting roasted banana drip down his chin. He smiled at Keisha with the most angelic smile and flicked his curly eyelashes at her, opening his big brown eyes wide.

"Razi, unstick yourself and go get my pink sweater off the line, please." Grandma smacked her lips and held the compact away from her face so she could see the whole picture.

"I'm getting chocolate marshmallow." Razi jumped from his chair and ran outside.

"Does this mean you're not coming with us to Mrs. Sampson's house, Mom?" Daddy's mind hadn't traveled to ice cream *or* puppies. It was still on the baby crow. "We might need you to convince her to let the crow go."

"Of course I'm coming, but not until after ice cream.

And I was talking about bringing Razi pie. Ice cream in a takeout box? In this heat?"

Grandma and Keisha looked at each other.

"Duh!" they both said at the same time, before giggling.

"Keisha, maybe you should make a temporary nest for our baby crow, one we can hang outside. That might help convince her. That crow needs to get back into the great outdoors as soon as possible."

"The one we really need is Jorge; he can give her the crow's point of view. And I already have the temporary nest," Grandma said. "Don't worry. We'll be there." Grandma rummaged in her purse until she found her seed pearl necklace. "I'm happy to go talk sense into Mrs. Sampson, but first I need my pie and then I need my ice cream. We were going to go out for them last night, but Cocoa needed a makeover."

"Cocoa?" Mama asked.

"Don't get your knickers in a knot, Fay. She's not a wild animal, so it's all right to name her. Cocoa's going to be someone's pet."

"What if they don't want to call her Cocoa?" Keisha thought it should be up to the person who adopted her to choose the dog's name. "What if they want to call her Fluffy? Or Sparkles?"

"I don't care if they call her Gabriella Louisa

Marchese Donatella Versace. As long as she goes to a good home."

No one got a chance to answer because Razi rushed through the back door, out of breath. "Somebody stole Grandma's sweater. We better call the police."

"Whoa, buddy, calm down and start over. It's not on the line? It was there when we were fixing the ducklings' enclosure." Daddy tugged the baby out of the high chair. Paulo was still dribbling.

"Fred, he's getting too big for that chair. Be careful." Mama released the tray.

"I saw it, too," Keisha said.

Sometimes things got stolen from the Carters' neighborhood. But not too many people wanted to come into a yard with so many wild animals—even if they were caged.

"Maybe it blew away."

"Well, there was enough wind to fly a kite, but I doubt enough to fly a pink cashmere sweater. And there wasn't a breath of wind last night," Grandma said. "Let's go out to the scene of the crime and see what's what."

All was quiet as they passed the skunk enclosure. That was as it should be because skunks liked to sleep during the day. Keisha looked up at the wash line. There were the two laundry clips, just where she remembered them. Everyone was looking around—at the bushes and trees, anywhere a sweater might get snagged if it was blown away.

"Razi, are you sure you didn't have anything to do with this?" Mama asked. Everyone knew how much Razi loved soft things.

"Why does everybody blame me? Why doesn't anyone blame Paulo?"

With roasted banana drool all over his face and his chubby legs dangling, Paulo looked very innocent of the crime of misplacing Grandma's sweater.

"Because he can't climb the laundry pole yet," Grandma said, lifting up the branches of the yew bushes that grew beside the house.

The Carters kept looking. Keisha noticed the laundry pole cast a long shadow over the skunk pen. . . .

Wait a minute! What was that peeking out from underneath the den box Razi had made? Yes! It was a little flash of pink cashmere.

Keisha understood why a skunk would like a soft cashmere sweater, but skunks are only about twelve inches tall when they stand up, so how did the sweater get from the laundry line into the skunk pen?

"Razi, we're not mad. Did you tuck the skunk in bed last night? Did you give him a blankie?" she asked her brother.

"No!" Razi crossed his arms, frustrated.

Then how did the sweater get all the way to the skunk's box?

"Mama? Daddy? Grandma? You better come look."

"That is not my pink sweater," Grandma said when she saw the corner of fabric under the skunk's den box.

"No, not your pink sweater anymore, Alice," Mama said. "Razi Carter?"

"How come everybody thinks I did it? I know better. Now Grandma won't give me any ice cream."

"Well, I'll be," Daddy said.

Keisha followed the route the sweater would have had to travel to go from the laundry line to the den box.

"I don't think Razi did do it, Mama," Keisha said. "I think the skunk did it. Look . . . the box is pushed closer to the fence. There are the drag marks. And Razi's truck is rolled next to the box. . . ."

"Connect the dots for me," Grandma said. "And do it in a hurry because my whole outfit hinges on that sweater—and Bob will be here any minute!"

"I think the skunk pushed everything over to the fence. Then he climbed up the truck and . . . jumped from the truck to the box. After he was on top of the box, he could use his claws to climb the rest of the fence. From the top of the fence, he could reach the sweater."

"I want to try it!" Razi was on fire with the possibilities.

"And where, Ada, does a skunk learn how to do that?"

"And if he got that high," Daddy said, "why not just climb down the other side and run away?"

For one long moment, not a single member of the Carter family could think of anything to say.

"This is no ordinary skunk, Fred," Mama said at last.

"No. On the one hand, this doesn't make sense. On the other—"

Daddy paused, figuring it out. "It makes a lot of sense. Our skunk goes through the motions of spraying but does not spray and it knows how to use toys and boxes to get what it wants. Are you thinking what I'm thinking, Fay?"

"This is someone's pet."

"Yes!" Keisha said. The last piece of the puzzle fell into place. A pet wouldn't want to leave a warm box and fuzzy sweater and a bowl of food to get back to the great outdoors. This skunk wasn't used to being in the great outdoors at all.

"You're telling me that someone is crazy enough to make this skunk their pet." Grandma wasn't buying it. "And keep it in the house, like a . . . like—"

"Cocoa," Keisha said. "He's domesticated."

"Maybe he got lost," Razi said. "Maybe his people are looking for him right now!"

"We'll have to drive through the neighborhood around the community garden and ask," Mama said. "You can borrow my pink sweater, Alice."

Baby Paulo started to wiggle and Daddy put him against his chest. "We'll go this afternoon after Mrs. Sampson's. I hope we find an owner. If he's a pet like we think, we won't be able to relocate him into the wild."

"Some skunks like camping out and some skunks prefer hotels with pink cashmere blankets. Jeez Louis Vuitton," Grandma said. "Now I've seen everything."

Chapter 10

"Mrs. Sampson, on behalf of the United States Postal Service, I must advise you that making a postal box unsafe for a carrier to deliver the mail is an offense punishable by law." Mr. Sanders's shoulders returned to their normal position. "We're only human, you know."

Mrs. Sampson sat at the kitchen table, her hands folded in front of her. "But I have the baby bird in that box over there."

Just before they'd left for Mrs. Sampson's house, Razi had been invited to run through the sprinkler at the Vanderests', so the Carters were able to swing by and ask Wita if Jorge could come along. Now Keisha and Jorge stood shoulder to shoulder waiting to see what would happen next.

Mama stepped forward and put her hand on Mrs. Sampson's. "A chicken does not forget where it lays its eggs, Mrs. Sampson, even after the eggs are collected."

"But they didn't lay their eggs in the mailbox."

"It's a Nigerian proverb, Mrs. Sampson," Daddy said. "I think Fay means the crows will come back to the mailbox until they know differently."

Just to let everyone know he was still in the room, the baby crow squawked.

"Oh dear," Mrs. Sampson said, pushing up from the table. "I need to feed him again."

"No, Mrs. . . ." Jorge held up his finger so everyone would stay quiet. The baby crow squawked again.

"I don't think your bird is hungry," Jorge said. "I think your bird is sad."

"How can he know that?" Mrs. Sampson looked over her glasses at Daddy. "He's just a child."

"In my experience, children are better at understanding animals than adults, Mrs. Sampson. However, it might help you to think about it this way. . . ." Daddy paused, waiting for the right words to come to him. "Think of the bird as . . . lonely. Lonely for other crows."

The porch screen door slammed.

"Move aside, everyone," Grandma Alice said in her most important voice. "We have an emergency case and I need to consult the nurse."

Mama raised her eyebrows and glanced over at Daddy. They couldn't get Mrs. Sampson to give up the crow. Why would they be bringing another case here?

Big Bob followed close behind Alice holding a large brown box in his hands.

Alice stepped to the side and swung her arm like

they did in the infomercials she watched on TV. "Ta-da!" she said.

Big Bob set the box down on the table so everyone could see. Cocoa was lying on her side, her little bandaged leg sticking out at an uncomfortable angle. She moaned in pain but wiggled her bottom anyway, to show she was friendly.

"Fred, I know you have a list of volunteers that work

with dogs and cats, too, but I'll be darned if I can find it."

"It's on the hard drive, Grandma," Keisha said. "Go to the 'organizations' file, and choose the 'vet volunteers' file."

Grandma Alice gave Keisha one of those you-must-not-have-any-idea-where-I'm-going-with-this looks. "I'm quite sure it is, dear, but we were having problems with the system this morning."

"What problems?" Daddy wanted to know. "That's a brand-new computer."

This time Daddy got the look.

Every third or fourth word in the conversation, the crow in the corner let out a squawk.

"That little guy's going to need a cough drop," Mr. Sanders said.

All of a sudden, there was a tremendous scuffling noise inside the box. The baby crow was trying to fly! He succeeded in lifting the tea towel a couple of times, but mostly, he sounded like he was knocking up against the sides of the box.

"What's happening?" Mrs. Sampson's open hand hovered over the box as if she could stop the little crow from hurting himself. "Why is he so upset?"

"He's doing what he is meant to do, Mrs. Sampson," Mama said. "He is trying to fly."

"I let him do that yesterday afternoon. We practiced launching off the kitchen table. But he could hurt himself in the box."

"You're right. He could injure himself." Daddy reached down and used the tea towel to scoop up the bird and pin its wings to its sides. "The first thing to know about wild animals, Mrs. Sampson, is that they won't do things on your timetable. He's not going to practice flying like Keisha going to the playground and practicing her double unders. He's going to do it whenever he wants."

The baby crow fell silent in Daddy's hands, making it easier to hear the moaning sound coming from the box on the table. Jorge was tall enough to see inside, but Keisha had to climb onto a kitchen chair to get a better view of the two button eyes and the little wet nose.

"What do we have here?" Mama said. "This does not look like a wild animal to me, Alice Carter."

"Now don't get your tea towels in a tangle, Fayola," Alice said. "I just wanted to consult the nurse."

"She's had a lot of tendon damage to her foreleg," Bob said.

"What kind of damage?" Mrs. Sampson asked, squinting into the box.

"Not sure. Definitely some sort of tear, but we're

also wondering about compression of the nerve endings and how that will affect her ability to walk."

"So she'll need this cast for a few weeks."

"At least. She has to have vitamins and antibiotics administered orally on a strict schedule and she'll have to be carried outside to go to the bathroom. After the cast comes off, she'll need physical therapy and to be walked with a sling until she can put weight on her leg. We're still not sure the leg can be used, but if she gets the right physical therapy, there's a chance."

"That's a lot of work for one old pup," Daddy said. "You're sure there's no owner?"

"Oh, this old gal has been on her own for some time," Bob said. "I agree, Fred. This is a hard case. Even if she does get the medical attention she needs, it won't be easy to find an owner for an old dog. They're just—"

"Daddy, I—" Keisha couldn't help herself. It just came out of her mouth. Wouldn't it be perfect? She could help rehabilitate this little dog, and then instead of releasing her into the wild, they could release her to the Carter family couch.

"I see where you're going with this." Mrs. Sampson was looking directly at Grandma. "But I can't take care of a crow and a dog."

"While the Humane Society does have a shortage of volunteers to take care of high-needs dogs, we do have two volunteers to watch over this crow." Daddy pointed to the front door. "And they're waiting in a tree outside. Jorge, do you think you can provide some evidence of this to Mrs. Sampson? We'll have to go out on the front porch."

"But can we leave the dog alone?"

"Oh, she's as comfortable as she can be, Mrs. Sampson," Grandma said.

Jorge, Mr. Sanders, Mama, Daddy, Grandma, Big Bob and Mrs. Sampson gathered together on Mrs. Sampson's front porch. They stood quietly, looking at the trees.

"First, let's get their attention," Daddy said to Jorge. "Why don't you sprint over to the mailbox?"

Jorge ran across the yard, stopping about ten feet from the mailbox. Up in the trees, the crows came alive. They didn't dive down on Jorge, because he wasn't close enough to endanger their baby, but they sure did put up a racket.

"I'm inviting them to my next New Year's Eve party," Grandma said. "They'll do a much better job than pots and pans of making a hullabaloo when the ball drops in Times Square."

"Okay, go." Quick as a wink, Daddy uncovered the baby crow's head and held him, pointing in the direction of the trees. Jorge began making his noises, only this time they weren't loud throat noises, they were little awping baby crow noises. The birds got very agitated. They circled Jorge and dropped down to branches closer and closer, responding in vocalizations Keisha had never heard crows make before. They were longer drawn-out caaaaaaws.

The baby crow struggled in the towel, but Daddy had him wrapped up tight. Except for his head. His glossy little head with the rock candy eyes turned this way and that, looking out at the big wide world.

"Awp, awp!" As soon as he started making noise, Daddy covered his head and took him back inside. The adult crows seemed confused. One landed right on the mailbox and pecked at it. Another soared to a tree closer to the porch.

"We don't need mama and daddy dive-bombing your front porch, Mrs. Sampson. Now do you see?"

Mrs. Sampson took off her glasses and polished them with her apron.

"I suppose we could give it a try," Mrs. Sampson said at last. "But my old eyes won't be able to keep track of him if he's not right in front of me."

Daddy patted Mrs. Sampson's shoulder. "You don't have to worry about that, Mrs. Sampson. We weren't able to build a nest with all that was going on this morning, but maybe we can rig something that will keep him protected until he's ready to be on his own. As you can see, his crow family stands ready to protect him."

"We don't have to rig a thing," Grandma said. "I came prepared. Keisha, go out to Bob's car and bring me what's on the backseat, please."

Keisha ran out to the car, taking care not to go anywhere near the mailbox. She opened the backseat door only to find Grandma's straw bag, the one she used to carry sunblock and swim caps to the pool. Surely she couldn't be thinking . . . Keisha brought the bag into the house.

"That's it, one ready-made crow nest."

"But this is your favorite pool bag," Mama protested.

"Correction, it *was* my favorite pool bag. According to Marilyn Kirschner of The Look On-Line, straw bags are seriously OL. I want to re-purpose this bag to be a baby crow sling." Grandma squinted and put her hand to her forehead like a visor.

"Look out there. We can hang him on the laundry line. He'll be in the shade, and it's not too far from the ground for when he's ready to flutter."

"Alice, you've really thought this through."

Grandma Alice rummaged in her purse and pulled out the scissors from their kitchen drawer.

"Yes, I have," she said. "I put a Tupperware top in

the bottom to make sure it doesn't collapse and we're going to have to cut down the sides a bit for easy re-entry. Believe me, given the crows' nests I've seen, this little baby is getting the Cadillac version."

"Let's hang this," Daddy said, examining the bag. "And if it works as well as I think it will, Mrs. Sampson can give it back to us after the crow abandons it. Now, I don't know about the rest of you"—Daddy was rubbing his stomach—"but I might need a little something to tide me over until dinner. I can run over to Charley's candy store and get some fuel for the volunteer cat chasers."

"Oh dear," Mrs. Sampson said, glancing toward the kitchen. "Children don't need candy for fuel. I—Misty, my niece, had the flu and couldn't take me grocery shopping."

"I took the liberty already," Grandma said, "when I noticed you were a little low. Bob's got the cooler in his trunk. You can't travel with this crowd and not bring food along. I bet even the little one could use a snack before we hang him out to fly."

Alice and Bob went out for the cooler, Jorge seemed happy outside with the birds and everyone else went back into the dining room. Wumpa-wumpa-wumpa. Cocoa's tail against the side of the box greeted them as they walked into the room.

Carefully, Mama picked up the little dog. Cocoa's front leg hung straight down in her cast. Some hair had been shaved away on her behind. Keisha counted seven stitches.

Mama turned Cocoa in such a way that there was

no pressure on her wounds. Cocoa would have licked Mama, but she had to lick the air instead. Still, Keisha couldn't believe her eyes. Mama didn't like dogs very much. Or at least that's what she said. Now she was cuddling Cocoa and making the little crooning noises she made to Paulo.

Mrs. Sampson leaned in, peering at the incision. "It's more a tear than a cut. Could this little dog have been in a fight?"

"That's something we'll never know," Daddy replied. "Maybe she crossed to the wrong side of the street into a bigger dog's territory."

Mama kept crooning.

Mrs. Sampson fingered the cast. "And what did you say this one was? A boy or a girl?"

"A girl," Daddy said.

Mrs. Sampson patted the dog's head. "What's her name?"

"We don't name our patients, Mrs. Sampson."

"But, Fred, this is not our patient," Mama corrected him. "Cocoa, I believe."

"Well, that would make sense," Mrs. Sampson said. "Her fur looks like a cup of nice hot cocoa."

Alice and Big Bob "pardon me'd" their way past Cocoa's admirers into the kitchen.

"So, Bob," Mama said as Big Bob returned to the dining room. "What will happen to this little one?"

"Can't say. Our other foster homes are full up. Half of the volunteers are on vacation. Cocoa's going to need someone to watch this incision and—"

"Someone with training, not just anyone," Mrs. Sampson interrupted. She was still examining the wound.

"Yes, exactly. And that someone's going to have to put salve on her wounds and carry Cocoa outside for a while."

"Well, I'm a little old for that sort of thing," Mrs. Sampson said.

"She's light as a feather," Mama said, handing her over to Mrs. Sampson before the old woman could protest. "Not more than twelve pounds."

"Well." Mrs. Sampson held the trembling little dog. "Well. She is a little thing."

"The sad part is," Bob continued, "even if her leg heals up, she's still going to have problems. That's my guess, and I'm afraid we won't find a home for her."

"You can't get old without having problems. I'd like to see the old person who doesn't," Mrs. Sampson said.

"Yes, well, we'll take her back now. I can keep her overnight, but when I have to go to work—"

"Maybe if the little crow finds its way, I could do the looking after. I don't have good eyes, but my hands are still strong. And I can use the magnifying glass to put on the salve."

"That would be a mission of mercy, for sure,"

Grandma said, coming in with a platter of cold cuts, cheese, lettuce, bread and juicy ripe sliced tomatoes. "And if you need some volunteers to run around with her when she gets her cast off, I can think of two named Razi and Keisha Carter."

Chapter 11

Razi loved fires. Grandma Alice said he danced around them just like Rumpelstiltskin. It wasn't legal to have a campfire in your backyard in the city, but you could have one in a fire pit. Two summers ago, the Carters dug a big hole in the side yard and lined it with stones. On special occasions, they got to roast s'mores outside, using sticks they cut from the box elder trees that grew in the alley.

Tonight, in celebration of releasing the baby crow into the wild—and finding a nurse for Cocoa—Zack, Zeke, Razi, Keisha, Grandma and Big Bob were making s'mores. Paulo was sleeping in his crib with the baby monitor at the window, and Mama and Daddy had walked over to Genny's Diner, home of the best frickled pickles and sweet daddy fries in Grand River.

"Look who I found." Big Bob rode into the yard on his old bike. He was a little out of breath because he was pedaling with Jorge on the seat. "We were researching the call of the red-breasted nuthatch this morning and we just so happened to enter 's'mores' into the search engine. Wait until you see this." Big Bob unzipped his backpack and started fishing around.

"Jorge!" Razi ran over and hugged his new friend. "Do you still have my flower eraser?" Ever since Jorge rescued Razi from the "pig nose incident," Razi loaned things to Jorge. That was one way Razi showed how much he liked someone. The other was to stand next to him, tug on his sleeve and whisper into his ear a lot.

Jorge pulled the eraser out of his pocket. "I've only erased with it a little," he said. "One drawing."

"Good." Razi squeezed Jorge's hand. "I'll take it back now." He fished around in his pocket. "But you can borrow my marble if you want."

Jorge took Razi's marble. "A cat's-eye. Thanks. I'll give it back."

"Gentlemen, ladies, Jorge and I found some new technology we would like to introduce this evening to enhance the roasting experience. Alice, drumroll, please."

Grandma slapped her hands on her thighs. Jorge joined in, using his pointer and middle fingers as drumsticks on the trash can lid they used to cover the fire pit when it wasn't being used. That felt more like a drumroll.

Big Bob pulled a handful of wire coat hangers out of his backpack.

"That's it?" Zeke asked. "I thought it would be something you could plug in. Or at least something with batteries."

"Yeah, like a marshmallow rotisserie," Zack added.

"Oh, this is so much better. With these babies, you can control the burn. You are in 'char' of your own experience. Portable, reusable. No batteries required. Gentlemen, ladies, be prepared for a s'more beyond your wildest imagination."

Razi, Jorge and the Z-Team got into bending wires with Big Bob, but Keisha thought she would stick to her box elder branch.

"Want me to make one for you, Keisha? I'm good at this." Zack waved an unhooked-but-still-bent wire in Keisha's face.

Keisha's answer was interrupted by a loud, stinky pickup truck pulling into the alley.

"Jeez . . . what is that smell?" Zack waved his wire in front of his nose.

"Smells like rotten eggs," Zeke said.

"That's sulfur," Big Bob told the boys. "Hopefully, he won't stay long."

"It's the Farleys' daughter—Meghan—getting picked up by her new boyfriend. What is his name?" Grandma asked Keisha.

"Keith!" Razi loved to have the right answer. "He gives out peppermints, but only if you're with Mama or Daddy or Grandma."

"Keith. Right." Grandma pulled on both ends of her wire to straighten it. "I keep telling him that sulfur smell probably means he needs a new muffler."

Keisha sniffed. There was something familiar about that smell.

"Okay." Big Bob was still instructing. "Jorge is going to hand out the marshmallows. Now, rule number one: Don't poke the marshmallow all the way through."

"What if we want a double-decker?" Zack asked. "Two marshmallows."

"You have to do one at a time. This is gourmet. Right, Alice?"

"Sure." Grandma was rubbing her forehead. "I hope Keith picks her up and gets a move on. . . . That smell is giving me a headache." Big Bob leaned over and put a marshmallow on the tip of Grandma's wire.

"Grandma, that smells like the community garden did when Mr. Peters reported the skunk. If the skunk didn't make the smell at the community garden, who did?" Keisha asked as she tried to find the right position, not too close and not too far away from the flames. She sat on a little stump Daddy had cut and left by the pit for sitting.

"Maybe Keith has a plot at the garden, too. . . ." Grandma was twirling her marshmallow stick with the same intensity that she rocked the swing on their back porch.

"No." Keisha turned her marshmallow slowly,

thinking. "The smell was definitely coming from inside the shed."

"Well, if there's any smell like *that* coming from that shed, we'd better check it out—"

"Now pay close attention." Big Bob interrupted Grandma with some last-minute s'mores instructions. "These babies use the conductive heat of the wire to cook your marshmallow outside and in."

"We know it wasn't skunk spray," Keisha said.

Grandma kept up her twirling. "Well, it had to be something . . . Bob? Bob! I'm on fire over here! How'd that happen?"

Chapter 12

The next morning, Razi was finishing up his lost skunk posters, Mama was doing the breakfast dishes, Paulo was teething on a spoon dipped in honey and Daddy and Grandma were doing dinner prep.

"Hey, bucko." Daddy leaned over Razi's drawing. "I don't think that's right. Keisha, is that how you spell *skunk?*"

As the fourth-grade spelling bee champion at Langston Hughes Elementary, Keisha was called upon to settle any spelling issues in the Carter household.

"Keisha said it rhymes with *trunk!*"

"Well, you got the *unk* part right. It's just that's a *k* instead of a *c*."

"Cuh-cat." Razi smacked his crayon on the table. "I already did six of them!"

"But if you do this . . ." Keisha picked up the crayon and showed Razi how to draw a straight line that tickled the back of the *c*, making it look like a *k*. "You don't have to erase a thing."

Razi laid all his posters on the table side by side. Then he took the crayon and, with great concentration, drew a straight line up against every *c*.

"Excellent," Grandma said. "Razi, you are a skunk artiste. Every one of these looks like Stinky out there. You even got the scar on his nose just right."

"No naming the animals, Grandma." Mama had finished the dishes and was now sitting at the kitchen table sewing a patch on Razi's jeans.

"I wasn't naming him. I was describing. But what would be the big deal if we did name him? He's not wild."

"That's only a hypothesis."

"Well, even if he was, he'll never be wild again. His defense mechanism's been disconnected."

"Which is precisely why we don't want to become too familiar with him. We don't have room for residents." Mama made a knot and bit the thread.

"Why you think I'd take kindly to a stinky little fur ball who eats garbage and steals my clothes, I don't know."

"Well, it's time to find the little fur ball a home. We're heading out soon to the community garden to put up these signs. Keisha, run down and get the staple gun," Daddy instructed.

"Check out that smell at the community garden," Grandma said. "There's something rotten going on over there and we know it's not a skunk with a loose shooter."

"Can I use the gun? Can I shoot the gun, Daddy?"

Daddy picked up Razi so they could rub nose to nose. "Possibly," he said. "Under very controlled conditions."

Daddy always gave Razi what Grandma called "the benefit of the doubt," but Keisha wasn't so sure it was a good idea. The staple gun was very strong. You could get hurt using it.

The Carters agreed that Daddy, Razi and Keisha should go to the community garden. Grandma had a hair appointment and Mama needed to stay home to take care of the animals. When Daddy offered to take Paulo, Mama said she could feed the ducklings and clean the raccoon and skunk pens with a sleepy Paulo in his stroller.

When the Carters arrived at the garden, they found Mr. Peters sitting on a stool, watering his tomatoes.

Daddy shook Mr. Peters's hand. "Fred Carter," he said. "Carters' Urban Rescue."

"Albert Peters. Is that your original artwork, young man?"

"We're doing a lost and find," Razi said, holding out one of his flyers.

"Ahhh." Mr. Peters examined the flyers. "First we get rid of the skunk and now you want to bring it *back* again?"

"No, Mr. Peters," Keisha said. "We think the skunk is somebody's pet."

"Holy tomato. Now I've heard everything."

"I've examined it, Albert," Daddy said. "The skunk has been de-scented. That's what people do to skunks in the pet trade."

"Well, if he was de-scented, how do you explain the smell around the garden shed? I've got to blame something."

"I think we've fallen victim to a logical fallacy," Daddy said. "You saw a skunk and we all smelled the smell that has some of the same qualities as skunk odor, so we thought $A + B = C$: bad smell + skunk = skunk odor. But my wife, who has a very keen nose for animal smells, was not convinced from the beginning. And my daughter is a born detective. She smelled exhaust mixed with the smell of burning wood yesterday and was reminded of the smell here."

"So what you're saying . . ." Mr. Peters stood up slowly. As Grandma would say, his thinker had shifted into high gear. "Even though the skunk is gone, the smell goes on and on, because . . . what made it is still here. And when you're smelling gasoline and burning . . . goodness gracious, we might have something flammable on our hands."

Daddy and Keisha nodded. They'd already come to this conclusion.

"My son's in the fire department," Mr. Peters said,

"and he has told me more than once, when you have problems like this, you should let the professionals handle it."

"Do you really think we need the fire department?" Daddy asked. "For a smell?"

"Daddy! Daddy! You said I wasn't tall enough to put up the posters. Maybe the firemen will let us use their ladder."

"I don't think they'd need to bring the fire truck," Mr. Peters said. "Al's the fire prevention officer. Maybe the emergency response vehicle."

"That's even bigger!" Razi threw his hands up in the air and lost a couple of skunk flyers.

"Razi!" Keisha chased after them. She had the feeling Razi didn't know what an emergency response vehicle was. . . . She wasn't sure herself, but she guessed maybe it was more the size of an ambulance.

Mr. Peters pulled out his cell phone and pressed a button. "I have the fire department on speed dial," he said, putting the phone to his ear.

In no time at all, an SUV pulled up. Keisha was right. The emergency response vehicle was more like a normal-sized car or van. Razi might have been disappointed, but as it made its way down the garden lane—popping a couple of melons under its wide tires, yellow and green lights flashing—he shouted, "It's like the circus!"

"Why do I get the feeling that life with you is something of a circus?" Mr. Peters asked Daddy. "Want me to hold on to those flyers for a minute?"

"That would be nice . . . while we check out this vehicle." Daddy put Razi on his shoulders. The truck pulled up alongside the Peterses' garden and a junior version of Mr. Peters rolled down the window. "Hey, Dad. You got a tomato emergency or what?"

"Very funny. But be sure to take a few home with you to Dena. She loves my beefsteak beauties. Now, Al. Oh . . ." Mr. Peters remembered his manners. "I didn't introduce you all. This is Albert Peters the Third. My son, Al."

Al got out of the truck. He looked very official with dark aviator sunglasses and *GRFD* embroidered on his shirt pocket. "Nice to meet you," he said. And he shook everyone's hand. Keisha made sure to look him in the eye and return Al's handshake with a firm grip.

"Fred Carter. Actually, I'm a wildlife rehabilitator and we got called out here because of a problem with a skunk. We did find a skunk, but now we realize he couldn't have caused the problem."

Al took off his glasses and sniffed the air. "Smells like sulfur," he said. "It is a little like skunk smell."

"Yeah, but his stinker's on the blink," Mr. Peters said. "The skunk's, I mean."

"This is my daughter, Keisha," Daddy said. "She's the one who put it together."

Daddy looked at Keisha. So did everyone else. He was expecting her to go on with the story. Razi had squirmed back down to the ground. Even *he* was looking at Keisha. What if they'd brought the fire department out for no reason?

"I'm not sure this makes sense," Keisha said. "But last night, when we were making s'mores in the fire pit, there was something about the smell of Keith's truck and maybe the matches we used to get the fire going. It reminded me of the smell in the garden shed. And I remembered that the skunk file said that sometimes people said skunk spray smelled like sulfur or burned rubber."

"A lot of other unpleasant things, too," Daddy added. "Rotting garbage, sewage—"

"And then . . ." Mr. Peters Junior looked at Keisha. He wanted to hear the rest of the story.

"And then," she said, hugging Razi close so he wouldn't launch into his own "and then" story. "I remembered that on the Fourth of July, Mama said the gardeners were picking up the papers from bottle rockets and firecrackers in their gardens. *And then* I remembered seeing some burned-up cherry bombs near the shed. And so when I told everything to Grandma

Alice, she suggested we come back to see if the smell is still here because it might be dangerous."

"I thought we were going to put up the lost skunk flyers," Razi said.

"Of course we are. We're multi-tasking." Daddy took Razi's hand. "I bet we could even find some late-bearing strawberries and, if we're nice, get a taste."

"Well, you called the right place. I am the fire prevention officer. When amateurs start investigating these things, someone could end up hurt."

"Believe me," Daddy said, "in our line of work, we know all about amateurs."

"So, where is this strange smell coming from?" Al asked.

"The garden shed. I'll lead the way." Mr. Peters marched them single file through the rows of bush beans and corn plants and honeysuckle vines to the garden shed.

"Whoo, I can really smell it here." Al took a long sniff. "Not quite gasoline. . . . You're right, Keisha. I smell sulfur, too."

They opened the shed door, and sunlight streamed into the dark cluttered space.

Al fell to the ground and started to crawl toward the back of the shed. "Stay back, everyone. Let the expert do the work."

All the Carters—Daddy had a firm grip on the back of Razi's shirt with his free hand—and Mr. Peters crowded into the doorway.

"Try not to block all the light," Al said. "What's this?"

Keisha could make out the dark outline of a machine. It looked a little like a lawn mower that had been cut in half.

"An old gasoline-powered tiller. I think it takes diesel fuel. One of the gardeners got it on Freecycle, that Web site where you give away old stuff."

It was hard to leave the doorway. Everyone wanted to know what Al was finding as he disappeared into the back of the big shed.

"Dad?" Al's voice came from the darkness. "When did this hay get put here?"

"I'd have to say last fall, when we needed some extra layers to protect against frost damage."

"There's residue. Something was lit . . . and it wasn't that long ago."

There was a long silence. Keisha's thoughts stretched back to the Fourth of July. Ping! Zing! Blam! In Grand River, people set off fireworks from mid-June through the first few weeks of August.

The group outside the shed waited silently for Al's diagnosis.

"Okay, then . . . *that's* stinky. Somebody call the undertaker. I've got the bottom half of a squirrel here. I'll give you the tail at no extra charge."

"I'm afraid that one's beyond our help," Daddy said. "But I do have some experience in carcass removal."

"I think that solves your mystery." Al had emerged from the dark shed and was blinking in the sunlight. "You have residue from illegal explosives. . . . I found some cherry bombs in there. As I'm sure you know, anything that spins, shoots up in the air or explodes is illegal in Michigan. But Indiana's only a couple hours away, and they have a cornucopia of exploding fireworks. We see it all summer long.

"Add to that, diesel fuel and some engine oil soaked into dry hay from a rusting tank on that tiller. Plus, one-half a squirrel carcass. Frankly, what you helped me discover, young lady, is an accident waiting to happen. If a lit match or an exploding firework got into that hay, this old shed would go up like a fireball. Good work. I'm going to recommend you as a candidate for our new JFPOT program."

"Jefpot?" Daddy said.

"Junior Fire Prevention Officer in Training, sir. It's a very important new branch of the fire department. This young lady could give a report on our findings."

154

Everyone clapped, which made Keisha cross her toes inside her tennis shoes.

Daddy waited until the applause died down. "It appears I have some work to do, too. I think I'll get some rubber gloves."

"That would be advisable." As they walked back to the Carters' truck, Al said to his dad, "What's that you've got there in your hand? You selling something?"

"Oh no. These are the flyers young Razi made to put up around the neighborhood. It seems that skunk we saw is somebody's pet."

"A pet skunk?" Al laughed. He took the poster from his father. "Wait a minute . . . a pet skunk. A pet skunk. Is this drawing accurate? Does he have a scar on his nose?"

"Yes!" Razi said. "I copied it."

"I guess it does." Daddy snapped on his rubber gloves.

"Well, guess what? I don't think your skunk is lost anymore. I know who owns this skunk. In fact, I rescued this skunk from a tree when it was a baby!"

"You're havin' us on, Al. You don't mean that."

Al straightened his GRFD badge and said: "As servants of the state of Michigan, we don't discriminate in rescue operations." He paused to put his

sunglasses back on. "Most people think we only rescue kittens, but we rescue anything that can find its
way up a tree and not back down, including Mrs. Tillie
Anderson of 1211 Sherman Oaks Boulevard, who was
hanging out Christmas tree lights and got paralyzed
with fright."

Chapter 13

Keisha and Razi hung out the window of the truck and watched as Daddy carried a pillowcase full of skunk to the lady Al Peters had just telephoned.

"Chester!" she said as she rushed out of her house.

"You seem to know this skunk, Ms. . . ."

"Downley. Cynthia Downley. I suppose I should check and make sure it really is our dear Chester."

"Probably a good idea."

Ms. Downley began to pull back the pillowcase opening and a furry head popped out, squinting in the sun.

"Chester. Oh yes, I can tell by this little scar on his nose. . . ."

"Where did that scar come from?"

"Oh dear. He got that launching himself from the butcher block into the pantry, where he ate half a box of Nilla wafers before I discovered him."

"So he *does* like Nilla wafers."

"And cashmere." Keisha poked her brother.

"Well, he likes them, but you might say they don't like him. He likes Oreo cookies even better, but they make him very sick. We had to stop keeping all chocolate in the house. Chocolate is deadly for skunks."

"Chocolate is deadly for a lot of animals, Ms. Downley. We've seen cases of chocolate poisoning in birds, a rat and a snake."

"It's very bad for puppies and older dogs, too," Keisha said from her spot at the window.

Ms. Downley turned and looked over at the truck. Then she nuzzled Chester. "We were so worried about you! He's usually not let into the mudroom because we have a cat door that leads to the outside. But someone must have forgotten. Wait!" She looked up. "We advertised a reward in the paper."

"No need for any reward, Ms. Downley. We are just doing our job." Daddy trotted back to the truck. Keisha had the business card ready. She handed it to Daddy. "However, if you feel like making a donation to Carters' Urban Rescue, you can underwrite the work we do with Chester's wild cousins."

Ms. Downley had gone back to rubbing her cheek against Chester's fur. "You little troublemaker," she said, as if she really didn't think he was a troublemaker at all. "Wait until the kids hear you're back."

She took the card from Daddy, thanked him again and hurried into the house, calling out: "Kids! Kids! Turn that TV off and come see what I've got."

"While we're out, can we check up on Mrs. Sampson and Cocoa?" Keisha asked. "We could give her some of Mr. Peters's tomatoes."

"Maybe she'll make us grilled cheese and tomatoes for lunch," Daddy said.

"I don't like tomatoes," Razi said.

"Then how about a grilled cheese and tomato sandwich, hold the tomato?" Daddy offered.

"I don't like to hold them, either."

"Well, then, give them to me. I'll salt them and save them for supper. We'll stop at Wolfgang's on the way home and you can get your grilled cheese straight up."

"But I don't want it straight up. I want it lying down."

The talk about sandwich fixings continued until they pulled into Mrs. Sampson's driveway.

"Well, look who's here," Mrs. Sampson said as she opened the door to them. "I was just making some lemonade for Jorge. I hope you don't have any more injured animals, because I've got my hands full!"

The Carters stepped through the hall into the dining room and saw Cocoa on the table. Mrs. Sampson had cut down the sides of the box so that Cocoa could see out. The little dog was wriggling around in the box the best she could. Grandma had given Mrs. Sampson the pink cashmere sweater, and Keisha could see that there were other blankets underneath the sweater, making a nice cozy nest for Cocoa.

"We're just finishing up lunch. I added some protein powder to a little boiled hamburger and rice. When I mash it all together, she can't get enough."

"Where does she eat?" Razi asked. "On the kitchen table?"

"Well . . . not exactly." Mrs. Sampson looked a little embarrassed. "I put the box on my lap and let her lick it off a spoon. She can't support her own weight yet."

Daddy patted Cocoa's head and let his hand travel down the dog's body. "I'd say she's gained a pound already, Mrs. Sampson. You are a good nurse."

"Well, it's important for patients to be comfortable," Mrs. Sampson said, brushing some crumbs off the table and bustling over to the garbage can. "Safe and clean and comfortable and then the appetite returns. I've seen it many times."

"Where's Jorge?" Keisha asked.

"In the potter's shed."

Razi and Keisha went to the front door and looked out. They could see the laundry line where Grandma's straw purse swung empty in the breeze. They could see the grape arbor where the Z-Team and Keisha first hid from the crows, and they could see the mailbox where the baby crow was first hidden. Where was the potter's shed?

"There he is," Razi whispered, as if calling out would attract the attention of the dive-bombing crows. Tucked into some bushes behind the laundry pole was a little shed, just big enough for one person to stand inside. But Jorge wasn't standing. He was sitting on an upside-down peach crate, his chin resting on his knees. He was looking out onto the yard. Keisha wondered if he was seeing something they couldn't. She waved her arms to get his attention. Jorge waved back.

"I wonder where the baby crow is," Keisha said.

"Do you think he flew away?" Razi sounded sad.

"That's what he's supposed to do, Razi." Keisha put her arm around her little brother.

As if to answer Razi's question, Jorge got out of his seat and put something in Grandma's straw purse. When he got back to the shed, he made a few crow noises. The noises sounded like a cross between a caw and an awp.

Keisha heard rustling in the trees. At first, nothing happened. Then crackle, snap, almost like falling, but not quite. In a flutter of wings, the little crow landed in Grandma's purse. He pecked around the bottom until he found the treat Jorge had left.

The crow looked around for a moment; he seemed

to be looking right at Jorge. Then he flew back to the shelter of the trees. There was more rustling and snapping and Keisha could tell there were other crows in the trees, too. They were hard to see, though, especially when they didn't make any noise.

Keisha and Razi went back into the house. Mrs. Sampson was sitting beside Daddy, Cocoa's box balancing on her lap.

"What will happen to Cocoa, do you think?" Keisha whispered to Daddy. "Will anyone adopt her?"

"I think someone already has," Daddy whispered back.

"But pets cost a lot of money." Keisha looked around at the cracked plates and the jelly jars. She wasn't sure Mrs. Sampson had that kind of money.

Mrs. Sampson tickled the ruff of fur at Cocoa's neck as the dog took her after-hamburger-and-rice nap.

"I know what you're thinking, Keisha, but Mr. Sampson and I didn't spend a lot of money. We were Depression babies and that meant we learned to make do with what we had. I have enough money. Mr. Sampson left me well provided for."

Suddenly Mrs. Sampson teared up and Keisha reached over to get a tissue for the old woman. "Well, he couldn't have provided for the loneliness, but this old thing"—she picked up the whole box on her lap and squeezed it—"might ease the pain."

She sat back in her chair and sighed. "Jorge and I have been talking, too. . . . Well, I've been talking to him. That boy is not much of a talker. But our thought is to set up a bird-feeding station here. Then he can really learn more about this hobby of his, and it will help me pass the time during the winter."

"That's a great idea," Keisha said. Her mind cast back to the day before when she and Grandma and Mama and Paulo had sat in the warm dozy kitchen. It was just about midday now, and it felt warm and dozy in here, too. Razi was stacking napkin rings, one on top of the other, and Daddy and Mrs. Sampson were talking quietly. Chester the skunk had been found, and Jorge was outside watching after the baby crow.

Everything felt just right. Keisha tiptoed over to the sleeping Cocoa and, very gently, drew in the dog's fur the words "The End."

From the Skunk Fact File

• Skunks are mammals similar in size to cats. They live about 3 years in the wild and up to 15 years as domestic pets. City parks, empty lots and abandoned buildings can all be homes for skunks.

• Skunks don't like to fight or bother others. They will only spray when they feel threatened. The spray comes from two glands beneath the tail. Skunks can spray up to 25 feet!

• All in all, skunks are good members of the animal community. They eat a lot of bugs we don't like and keep to themselves. A good skunk motto is "Live and let live."

• Some people choose to keep skunks as pets. To understand the joys and challenges of owning a skunk as a pet, visit the Web site www.skunkhaven.net.

From the Crow Fact File

• Crows are big, glossy-feathered black birds that grow to be about 16 to 20 inches long. If they survive their first year of life, crows can live to be 7 to 8 years old in the wild and 17 to 20 years old in captivity, though the oldest crow was 59 years old!

• Since crow babies are big, people often think they are injured when they can't fly. You can tell by watching the bird closely. Can it move around and balance on its own? If so, then it is still learning. Unless it is in immediate danger from a cat or a car, please leave it alone. Most likely its parents are nearby.

• Crows are very social animals, and if they are kept away from crow society while they are young, they might never be accepted back into it.

• Crows swoop down on cats, dogs and even kids to protect their babies. After a few days, when their babies have learned to fly, they stop this behavior.

WHATEVER THE DILEMMA, IF IT'S GOT FUR OR FEATHERS

THE CARTERS ARE THE ONES TO CALL!

FROM THE DESK OF
SUE STAUFFACHER

Dear Readers,

   In honor of this book, my German shepherd mix, Sophie, got sprayed by a skunk she found in our yard. Ugh. It is a hard smell to describe. Add one cup of burning wood to one cup of rotten garbage to two cups of rotten egg and you'll be getting close. After trying lots of homemade recipes (which all worked a little), we went to the pet store and got an odor-neutralizing product. That was the best thing.

   Two crow families also decided to build nests in our yard and raise their young while I was writing this book. I know because Mama and Papa Bird got hopping mad when I walked anywhere near that part of the yard, flapping their wings and cawing like crazy. It was fun to watch the baby crows get big and practice flying, but I don't know about living next door to them. They are noisy neighbors.

   Another thing writers say to each other is "Write what you know." Believe me, I know skunks and crows!

Happy reading!
Sue

Acknowledgments

I want to thank all my readers on the Animal Rescue Team for spreading the word about how to keep wild animals wild and safe. I also want to thank the educators who help us learn by sharing their knowledge on the Web. For example, Kevin McGowan is a behavioral ecologist at the Cornell Laboratory of Ornithology. He has studied crows for twenty years and shares his findings with us at www.birds.cornell.edu/crows. Thank you, Kevin! Another of my favorite Web sites for helping kids know what to do when they encounter wildlife in their own backyard is the Humane Society's Wild Neighbors page: www.humanesociety.org/animals/wild_neighbors/

Most of all, a big thank-you to the wildlife rehabilitators themselves. These dedicated professionals work long hours to help animals in need. To find a good wildlife rehabilitator in your area, you can contact your state's department of natural resources office or your local zoo, veterinarian or animal shelter.

About the Author

Sue Stauffacher lives with her husband and sons in a 150-plus-year-old farmhouse in the city of Grand Rapids, Michigan. Over the years, possums, bats, raccoons, mice, squirrels, crows, ducks, woodchucks, chipmunks, voles, skunks, bunnies and a whole bunch of other critters have lived on the property. Though Sue is not a rehabilitator herself, she is passionate about helping kids know what to do when the wild meets the child.

Sue's novels for young readers include *Harry Sue, Donutheart* and *Donuthead*, which *Kirkus Reviews* called "touching, funny, and gloriously human" in a starred review. Her most recent picture book, *Nothing but Trouble*, won the NAACP Image Award for Outstanding Literary Work—Children. Besides writing children's books, Sue is a frequent visitor to schools as a speaker and literacy consultant, drawing on two decades of experience as a journalist, educator and program administrator. To learn more about Sue and her books, visit her on the Web at www.suestauffacher.com.